AWESOME
Wildlife
DEFENDERS

AWESOME
Wildlife
DEFENDERS

martha attema

RONSDALE PRESS

RONSDALE PRESS
3350 West 21st Avenue, Vancouver, B.C. Canada V6S 1G7
www.ronsdalepress.com

Typesetting: Julie Cochrane, in Minion 12 pt on 16
Cover Design: Julie Cochrane
Paper: 100 Edition, 60 lb. offset white paper (FSC) — 100% post-consumer
    waste, totally chlorine-free and acid-free

Ronsdale Press wishes to thank the following for their support of its
publishing program: the Canada Council for the Arts, the Government of
Canada, the British Columbia Arts Council, and the Province of British
Columbia through the British Columbia Book Publishing Tax Credit program.

Library and Archives Canada Cataloguing in Publication

Title: Awesome wildlife defenders / Martha Attema.
Names: Attema, Martha, 1949– author.
Identifiers: Canadiana (print) 20210134321 | Canadiana (ebook) 2021013433X
    | ISBN 9781553806479 (softcover) | ISBN 9781553806486 (HTML) | ISBN
    9781553806493 (PDF)
Classification: LCC PS8551.T74 A96 2021 | DDC jC813/.54–dc23

At Ronsdale Press we are committed to protecting the environment. To this
end we are working with Canopy and printers to phase out our use of paper
produced from ancient forests. This book is one step towards that goal.

Printed in Canada by Island Blue, Victoria, B.C.

To Femke, Mia, Allie, Klazina,
Alexander and Loesje.
You are my inspiration.
You are the future!

"You aren't going to save the world on your own. But you might inspire a generation of kids to save it for all of us. You would be amazed at what inspired children do."

— JANE GOODALL

ACKNOWLEDGEMENTS

I would like to thank the following people, whose support has made this book possible:

Ann Featherstone, for her suggestion to rewrite the chapter book version of this story and make it suitable for middle-grade readers.

Penny Lecour, for sharing my passion to teach our grade one students about endangered species.

Heather Stemp, for reading several versions of this work in progress. Her advice, guidance, enthusiasm and friendship mean much to me.

Karen Upper, school librarian, for reading an early draft of this story and giving feedback, for organizing the Forest of Reading celebrations and introducing many authors to our students.

Rebecca Upjohn and Frieda Wishinsky, your stories are inspirational. I'm grateful for your friendship.

Ronald and Veronica Hatch, Publishers, for taking on my story and for their editorial advice and guidance.

Hélène Leboucher, for her suggestions and for answering all my questions.

Megan Warren, for noticing the small details.

My family for their love and support.

In memory of my dear friend and fellow writer, Marla J. Hayes. For over thirty years she has encouraged me to get my stories published and to never give up trying.

AWESOME
Wildlife
DEFENDERS

Chapter 1

"WHERE'S MR. R?" I yelled at Frieda. I tried to cover my ears as the noise level in our grade five class got higher and higher. "Do you think something happened to him?" Strands of my long blond hair stuck to my face and got in my eyes, and suddenly it was too much to handle with all of the noise. I uncovered my ears for a second to frantically check my jeans pockets for an elastic. At that moment, I knew that this day was not going to be great.

"Don't know," my best friend yelled back. "He's always on time."

My classmates were going bananas. The chaos was deafening. My chest felt tight, and my stomach churned. It felt like a roaring noise wrapped around my brain. I had named my panic attacks *thunderbolts.* They appeared suddenly, like lightning strikes, when I found myself in unexpected situations, in large crowds or surrounded by loud noises. I put my head on my desk. With my arms wrapped around my ears, I waited. But nothing dampened the squeals, shouts and table-banging going on around me. Soon, some of the other students would probably make fun of me.

I didn't always have these attacks. They started when I was in grade three. One day, Mom and I were riding the city bus when a truck went through a red light and slammed into the side of the bus. Luckily, no one was seriously hurt, but we were in shock. That night, I had my first panic attack. It was awful. As I sat covering my ears amidst the classroom turmoil, I could almost hear the sound of the crash growing behind the other students' voices.

Frieda grabbed my arm. "Rebecca, are you okay?"

My friend worried about me too much. I was a head taller than her, but some days she treated me like her younger sister.

I nodded at Frieda and, as I looked up, the door burst open.

"Good morning, awesome Earth warriors and soon-to-be wildlife defenders!" Mr. R., our teacher, announced in a booming voice.

I felt uneasy as I watched him stride into the classroom and take off his backpack. He threw it like a bowling ball, watched it slide across the front of the room and smiled when it stopped right at his desk. His windblown dreadlocks were tangled in a nest, his glasses had slid down his nose and drops of sweat glistened on his dark forehead. I looked at his rumpled clothes and noticed that his shoelaces were undone, and I worried. What had happened to him?

"Wildlife defenders?" Eric jumped up and down. "Mr. R., you're crazy!"

Eric wasn't able to sit still for one second. He was always acting out and had an opinion on everything. I didn't like him at all. He constantly reminded me not to "trip over those lanky legs" or called me "skinny legs," as if I didn't know that my long limbs sometimes made me clumsy. And Ben totally agreed with him, always adding to Eric's insults by saying, "Don't get your tentacles in a knot!"

My teacher held up his arm and everyone quieted. He cleaned his glasses and put them back on. The pent-up air escaped from my lungs. My chest still hurt, and my stomach hadn't settled, but at least Mr. R. had arrived. Looking at the dishevelled state he was in, I longed to know what he would say next.

"He's sooo unpredictable." Frieda shook her head, which made her auburn curls dance. I loved the colour of her hair, the stars in her dark blue eyes and the pale freckles sprinkled on her face and arms. She hated her freckles and often told me that she wanted to cover them with makeup.

My breathing had found its rhythm, but my voice refused to respond. I nodded in agreement.

Our teacher panted, took a big breath and began his first rhyme of the day. *"I'm sorry I am late, which I did not antici-pate. My trustworthy bike got a flat. I had to run to school, faster than a racing cat."*

While I listened to his rhyming efforts, I continued to focus on my breathing and tried to remember what else I needed to do to calm my panic attack. I felt my anger rise, which didn't help. Why did a *thunderbolt* attack me every time something out of the ordinary happened? The attacks made me shy away from certain events and crowded places and they made me feel stupid. I never got used to the atten-tion and comments I had to endure from my classmates when they struck.

Frieda's kind face still watched me as I focused. Even her freckles were full of concern. "Are you going to be okay?"

I smiled weakly to reassure her that it would pass. It always did.

"Why don't you buy a car, Mr. R?" Eric asked. He was out of his seat again.

"Because Mr. R. doesn't want to pollute the air!" Ben slicked back his straight brown hair and rolled his eyes.

"An electric car would be good for the air," Eric added. "Not like Ben's dad, who owns a truck, an SUV, an old Mer-cedes from the 1950s and don't forget a sports car. My dad says they're all gas-guzzling polluters."

Ben and Eric were the two biggest pests. Ben was a show-off and thought he was some kind of hero because he lived in a mansion, and Eric liked to compete for attention. They drove me crazy.

"You are right, but . . . *As an Earth warrior, I try to be smart! Biking to work is how I do my part.*"

"Rhyme number two," Frieda whispered. "And where did he get that shirt? There are orangutans all over it."

"At the thrift shop," I whispered, glad to have found my voice. "The last time Mom and I went shopping, I saw him buying clothes there. I hid. I didn't want him to see me." To be honest, I didn't want anybody to see me in the thrift shop. I didn't want my teacher to know that we couldn't afford new clothes, or new anything. Mom and I had to be careful. As a writer, she didn't make much money. Gram, my mom's mother, sometimes helped us when Mom didn't get paid for a while. When she didn't want Gram to know that she couldn't afford food, we went to the food bank. I wasn't supposed to talk about it with anyone else. Frieda was the only one who knew because she'd been my best friend since kindergarten. Lately, we hadn't needed any help and I was glad.

"*I know you think I'm crazy,*" Mr. R. started rhyming again, "*but we cannot be lazy. When species vanish fast, they'll end up in the past.*"

My brow furrowed. "What's he talking about?"

"You mean rhyming about," Frieda chuckled.

Before she could say anything else, our teacher continued.

"*I bet you're dying to start. This environmental project will make you super smart.*"

"Another project," Jake groaned. "Too much work! And wasted paper and energy!"

"You're just lazy, Jake. We'll learn so much, right Mr. R.?" Bossy Brianna stood up and placed her hands on her hips. She smiled one of her famous sweet, fake smiles and raked her fingers through her spiked purple hair.

Jake rolled his eyes at her. "Teacher's pet!"

"Remember, I only have one pet," Mr. R. responded.

"*Friendly is your pet, we could not forget!*" Eric chanted, directing his own words with his arms as if he was conducting a symphony.

For once, Eric was right. We all loved Mr. R.'s mixed breed creature that looked more like a wolf than a dog. Mr. R. had saved him from a terrible fate when he rescued Friendly from the animal shelter last year. When the dog came to visit our class, he was so excited and affectionate that we all fell in love with him.

"Let's work on this project together," Frieda said, tapping my arm. "We can work at my place if your mom is busy writing and needs space."

"That sounds like a plan!" We high-fived. I loved going to her place. Frieda's four older brothers were funny, kind and big teasers. Her mom was crazy about gardening. Her dad drove one of those mega transport trucks all across the country. I usually counted at least four cats at her house.

Mr. R. swung around to the blackboard and wrote in big, messy letters: ENDANGERED SPECIES.

"Recently, the news reported that over the last forty years we have lost sixty per cent of all species. Sixty per cent is a huge loss, and that is why I chose this topic. *You'll work in teams of two, but,*" he peered over his thick, orange-rimmed glasses to see if we were paying attention, "*this time, your partner won't be picked by you.*"

I looked at Frieda, who gaped back at me. "NOOOO" we mouthed.

"THAT'S NOT FAIR!" Bossy Brianna screamed. "I only work with Violet! You know I can only work with Violet. And, by the way, nobody else in this class will want to work with me!" She took a deep breath and looked very smug, as if she was proud that no one wanted to work with her.

We all knew why she was friends with Violet. Brianna loved the free meals she got at Violet's parents' Vietnamese restaurant and Violet was so soft spoken that she would never stand up to Brianna.

I was glad that Mr. R. ignored Brianna's objection and raised his arm again. He walked over to the music centre. "Now I need you to listen. We're going to play a game to help you find your partner for the project."

These were not comforting words for me. Since classes had started in the first week of September, our teacher had made every activity into a game, and I didn't usually mind. But now, I was worried. If we couldn't choose our partner, who was mine going to be? I could end up with Brianna. I wanted to work with Frieda because she is my BFF, my Best

Friend Forever. I looked around the room and confirmed what I already knew. Frieda was the best partner to work with.

Before he pressed the button, my teacher raised his arm and announced, *"By the end of this game, you'll know your partner's name."*

A rap song about disappearing animals blared full blast.

I motioned for Mr. R. to turn down the sound. He did, but not before Brianna pointed at me.

He came over and knelt by my desk. "Sorry, Rebecca," he whispered. "In my excitement, I forgot that loud noises bother you. Please let me know immediately when I get carried away like that."

"Oh, Rebecca, you're such a baby!" Brianna blurted out. "Why don't you wear earplugs?"

I cringed but resisted the temptation to say something. It wouldn't change the way Brianna treated me anyway.

Chapter 2

NEXT, WE WERE TOLD to move around the room. It was impossible for Frieda and me to stay together, even though I tried desperately to follow her closely. Mr. R. separated us and pointed us in different directions.

By now, I had already figured out that we'd have to work with the person we ended up standing beside when the music stopped. My heartbeat accelerated and I feared another *thunderbolt*. The first one had barely subsided. Across the room, Frieda rolled her eyes and made a face at Brianna. Oh no, I thought. If those two end up together, there'll be fighting for sure.

And then the music stopped. I closed my eyes and focused

on my breathing for a moment before I turned to find out who my partner was. When I opened them, I was standing beside Cedar.

Cedar didn't look at me, he just stared at the floor. I couldn't see the expression on his face, but his eyes were dark and sad. I didn't want to work with him and I'm sure he hated being teamed up with a girl, too.

Cedar always wore homemade clothes, had longer hair than any of the girls in the class and lived with his grandfather. He had been in my class since grade one, but he kept to himself. In all four years I'd never heard him speak. In grade three, his grandfather came to our class and taught us how to make drums. I remember him teaching us about Mother Earth's heartbeat and our own heartbeat with the beat of the drum.

I wanted to sink into a hole and disappear or, better yet, crawl across the floor and end up next to Frieda. I put my hand over my mouth, trying not to hyperventilate. As I slowly calmed down, my eyes wandered around the room to check out the other teams.

Frieda ended up with Brianna, just as I feared. That was not going to be a good partnership.

Violet ended up with Karen. They were both super quiet. Maybe after they did a project together, they could become friends and Violet could get rid of Brianna.

Marla and Kadidja were a good team. Kadidja was a refugee from Africa and was new to our class. She was very pretty, and her skin was even darker than our teacher's. Every day she wore a different headscarf. She struggled with her new language. Marla had problems with her feet and used a walker. She was very smart, because she always had her nose in a book. They would be a strong team.

The boys were all in pairs, except for Cedar. Great! Cedar and I were the only girl-boy team! Now Bossy Brianna would have another excuse to make fun of me — of us. Eric would have another reason to make snide remarks and Ben would have a blast adding his stupid comments. This just wasn't fair! How was I supposed to work with someone who had never spoken a word in class, who never participated and who kept to himself? My breathing quickened and I grabbed the nearest desk for support. My stomach churned and twisted into a knot. I glanced desperately at Mr. R.

"Fantastic!" he hollered. *"The two of you must soon agree on which endangered species it's going to be."*

I couldn't believe it. How did he expect us to come up with an endangered animal when Cedar never talked to anyone?

"Tomorrow, I will give you time to work on your ideas together." He took a big gulp of air before he continued. *"Next Friday is the day that you'll finish your display — and have your say."*

"That's not enough time! Not even two weeks! Only *one* weekend to work on it!" Brianna shouted.

"Oh, c'mon, Brianna. You're highly intelligent. You don't need two weeks to pull this off!" Eric jumped up and laughed.

Mr. R. motioned for Eric to sit down. "I don't want you to spend that much time on this project. And I don't want this project to interfere with the Halloween activities I've planned for the last week of October."

Halloween. I sighed. Halloween activities would involve a lot of noise.

We all returned to our seats. I avoided eye contact with Cedar for the rest of the morning. Not that he was trying to get my attention, but just in case. The math problems we had to solve next seemed more complicated than usual and my brain struggled to sort out the number patterns.

On the way to the lunchroom, Brianna bumped my hip on purpose. "Sorry," she said with a mean smile. "I hope you and Mr. Birch Tree will have lots of fun with this project. I'm sure he'll talk your ears off." She laughed out loud at her own sarcastic remark before she ran ahead.

I felt angry and nauseated. The crackers and homemade hummus that Mom and I had made tasted delicious last night, but right now they looked inedible. I just drank my water.

"What are you going to do?" Frieda asked. The worry in her eyes was back.

"What can I do? Will anybody else volunteer to work with Cedar?"

"He doesn't talk to anybody! You need to talk to Mr. R." She bit into her egg salad sandwich and wiped the bread-crumbs from her pink sweater.

"And what will I tell him? That I can't work with Cedar?"

"Tell him that you'll have more panic attacks and that you'll feel better if you work with me. Brianna can work with him. She'll boss him around and make him do all the work."

"I'm not going to use my attacks as an excuse, and I'm sure Mr. R. won't go for that either." I shook my head at Frieda.

"You're right. But can you imagine working with Brianna? We both have a big problem, and I don't know what the solution is."

I totally agreed. There was Cedar, who wouldn't or couldn't talk, and Brianna, who wouldn't or couldn't *stop* talking.

When the final bell rang, Frieda and I walked to our bicycles. Mr. R. was standing with Cedar by the school gate, and they were actually talking. I wondered if Cedar was talking to him about working with me. Suddenly, he jumped on his bicycle and raced out of the schoolyard. Our eyes met for a split second, then I quickly looked away.

"Should we ride by Cedar's place?" Frieda suggested. "I know where he lives."

"Are you crazy? What if he sees us? He'll think we're spying on him."

"We *are* spying on him!" She jumped on her bike and rode away. I followed on my much slower, much creakier bicycle.

"He'll hear me coming from a mile away. My bike makes this grinding sound every time I pedal."

"Impressive sound, Rebecca!" Jake passed us on his skateboard.

I stuck out my tongue, but he just waved at me. Most of the students in our neighbourhood biked, walked or, in Jake's case, skateboarded to school. Three school buses picked up the kids who lived outside of our small Vancouver Island town. We waved at Marla, who was picked up by taxi.

"Follow me!" Frieda called as she turned onto Sparrow Street.

What was she doing? And, more importantly, why was I following her? It made me uncomfortable but, to be honest, I was also a little curious about where he lived. I hoped that Cedar and his grandfather were inside and away from the windows.

The houses on Sparrow Street had large front yards. Tall oak trees lined the sidewalks and covered the road in acorns that crunched beneath our tires. Most trees had already lost their yellow leaves in last week's storm and several home-owners were raking lawns and cleaning flowerbeds. I inhaled the scents of decay, of fall. The sounds of leaf blowers, dogs barking and children laughing drifted in and out as we passed by.

Frieda turned right onto Finch, a street with no exit. Near the end of the road, a log home with a red metal roof emerged from a cluster of trees.

"That's the house." She pointed. "Did you know he lived with his grandfather?"

"Yup." It seemed that Frieda always knew everything about everybody. "Where are his parents?"

"No idea." She shrugged.

I had never been at the end of Finch Street before. "Let's turn around!" I called.

Frieda looked at me over her shoulder and shook her head. "Let's just pedal past the house before we turn around!"

A large cedar hedge separated the property from the road. Two wooden bald eagles on posts guarded the entrance to their front yard.

"Cedar's grandfather is a woodcarver." She pointed at the eagles. "He must have carved those huge birds."

I liked how the light made the eagles' eyes come alive. They looked so real.

We turned around at the dead end and rode back side by side.

"Wow, did you see those other carvings? The grey wolf by the pathway is so lifelike," my friend raved. "I heard his grandfather is an amazing artist."

"I didn't see the wolf, but I loved the eagles." I had been too afraid to look directly at the house in case they saw me. "Did you notice anybody?"

Frieda shook her head. As we left Finch Street, we slowed down. "What are you going to do about Cedar?"

"I have no idea. I guess I'll wait 'til tomorrow, when Mr. R. gives us time to work together, and hopefully he'll help us. I saw him talking to Cedar before we left school. What will you do?"

"I guess I'll do the same." Frieda picked up speed. "Let's

hope Mr. R. will talk to Brianna before she gets too bossy with me."

I smiled. "If you can handle four older brothers, I think you can handle her."

"But Brianna on a good day is worse than all my brothers together on a bad day!"

At Nightingale Street, Frieda turned and I went straight. I made a right on Robin Court and stopped in front of my small, blue, metal gate, the entrance to our cozy little rental house. I parked my bicycle in the shed, lifted my backpack off the carrier and walked around to the front door.

Chapter 3

"IT'S NOT FAIR, MOM!" I threw my backpack down in the hallway, kicked off my shoes and flung my jacket to the hook, which of course I missed.

"It can't be that bad." Mom tucked a strand of blond hair that had escaped her ponytail behind her ear and pulled her oversized plaid shirt down over her leggings. Even in her messy writing clothes, I thought she looked beautiful. We had the same hair colour, but sadly the resemblance ended there. My eyes were greenish and Mom's were brown behind her glasses. Mom's nose was cute like a button, but mine was straight and much bigger, not cute at all. I looked her straight in the eye, something I could finally do since I was only slightly shorter than her. At least there was one perk to being tall for my age.

"Mo-om! Cedar is weird. He doesn't talk. He wears home-made clothes. Frieda said his grandfather has long hair like Cedar's and he's the one who sews all their clothes!"

"And you, Rebecca Brooks, listen to what other people say? I'm very disappointed. First of all, you don't know these things. Secondly, none of those things are bad. I think he sounds very interesting. Thirdly, Cedar has been in your class since grade one. He must have done well in school so far, or he wouldn't have made it to grade five. And finally, you say you *can't* work with him, or do you mean you *won't* work with him?"

"Both! Frieda and I always work together. She never makes me feel bad when I have an attack. I don't know how to work with him." Tears threatened to spill, but I didn't let them. "I can't work with anybody else." I stomped my feet so Mom knew I meant it.

"If everybody in your class has the same attitude, I don't blame your teacher for playing that game." She turned away and started clearing the table.

"Now you're on Mr. R.'s side! You're *my* mother! You should help *me*!"

She stayed silent. I didn't know what else to say either, but I couldn't stand her or the silent treatment she always gave me when we got into an argument and she was convinced that she was right.

After a while, I caved in and broke the silence. I always did.

"How are the vampires?"

Not only does my mother write about vampires, but I suspect she is one herself. She writes at night, when it's dark and vampires are on the prowl.

"They're in trouble." She shook her ponytail. "They're trapped."

"They'll have to wait 'til midnight before you can save them," I said in a spooky voice.

Ding-dong. The doorbell. We both looked up. Nobody ever rang the bell at our house. Frieda always just walked in, and so did Gram. My grandmother lives across town, but she owns a little car and visits at least twice a week or whenever I ask her to come over or take us somewhere.

Mom raised her eyebrows. "I'll get that." She went into the hallway and opened the door.

"Hi! You must be Cedar."

My breath caught. Cedar was here, at my door?

"Would you like to come in?" Mom asked.

I couldn't hear whether he answered my mother, but suddenly he stood in the hallway. His face was flushed and his long, dark hair hung in a braid over his shoulder.

"Hi," he said.

"Hi," I answered. I was surprised to hear his voice. So he could talk, after all. Why did he never speak in class?

Without a word, Cedar hung up his coat and planted his sneakers on the mat beside the door.

"Come into our kitchen-office-living room." I stood up and pointed to a chair. "Our house is small."

He didn't respond.

"Mom, this is Cedar. Cedar, this is my mom, Heather." I knew it sounded awkward, but I didn't know what else to say. He just stood there.

"I'll make hot chocolate." Mom grabbed the kettle and filled it with water, then turned on the stove.

"I can't have dairy," he said softly.

"We use non-dairy milk. Is that okay?" Mom opened the fridge.

Cedar nodded.

"You can sit down." I gestured again to the chair and this time he joined me in the kitchen. We sat silently while Mom added hot water and milk to the cocoa. I didn't look at him, nor did I know what to say. When I peeked through my eyelashes, I noticed that Cedar was looking down at the table.

My mother placed the mugs in front of us and sat down. I blew on my drink, stirring the spoon around and around before I took a sip.

"How did you know where I live?" I blurted when I finally thought of something to say.

"I asked Mr. R. for your address." Cedar took a sip.

So that's why they were together after school. Again, I wondered why he didn't speak in class. I assumed it was because he had no friends and kids like Brianna teased him about his name.

"Will you need to use my laptop for this project?" Mom asked, interrupting my thoughts.

I looked at Cedar.

"Thanks, that would help us with the research," he said with a small smile.

"Which endangered species did you choose?" she asked.

"We didn't." I put down my mug.

"I was thinking owls," Cedar said quietly.

"Owls?" I asked, surprised by his idea.

"Do you collect owls? Because I've seen your T-shirts and earrings and the owl patches on your backpack." He stared at his mug, which was decorated with an owl. I felt my cheeks burn in embarrassment. "I know the northern spotted owl is one of Canada's most endangered species."

He spoke in full sentences. And he knew I collected owls.

"What a great idea." My mother wiped her chocolate moustache with the back of her hand. "You should show Cedar your collection. Rebecca owns owl statues, earrings, T-shirts, sweaters, notepads, pens, pictures, cookie cutters, books on owls, a flock of stuffed owls and — "

"Mo-om!" Why did she have to embarrass me?

Cedar laughed. I'd never heard him laugh before. His laugh gurgled and made me and Mom laugh. It kind of broke the ice.

"I love the orca on your sweater," I said.

"My grandpa knit it."

"It's really good. It's so cool that your grandpa knows how to knit."

"I can knit, too, and sew. My grandma taught me, but she

passed away last fall." His voice trailed off and the sadness returned to his eyes.

"I'm so sorry." Mom looked at him. "You must miss her very much."

Cedar stared into his now-empty mug.

"We could do the killer whale instead," I suggested. "I know they're in trouble."

He shook his head. "Let's do the owl."

"Here." Mom placed her laptop on the kitchen table in front of us.

"Let's search the northern spotted owl. You can type it in." I opened the lid and pushed the laptop toward him.

When Cedar typed "northern spotted owl" into the search engine, websites dedicated to the species filled the screen. He clicked on the first link and we started reading. We were shocked to learn that there were fewer than thirty northern spotted owls remaining in our own province, British Columbia.

Next, Cedar scrolled through pictures of the spotted owls.

"Oh, look at the babies!" I cried. "They're adorable. They look like pompoms. Mom, can we print some of these pictures?"

"Sure," she answered.

We printed off our favourite photos of adult owls and owlets, then scrolled through the sections on habitat, food, appearance and why they are at risk. We took turns reading the sections out loud. Suddenly, I didn't find it strange that he was talking and reading the information to me. His voice was light and pleasant.

"Do you need to be home for supper at a certain time, Cedar?" Mom asked.

He looked at the clock above the stove. "Oh, I need to go. Supper's at six."

Six already? I hadn't realized how much time had gone by.

At the door, he pulled on his sneakers and pushed his arms through his jacket sleeves.

"Thank you." He smiled at Mom and me, then turned away.

Flabbergasted, I watched him hop on his bicycle and pedal down the street.

· · ·

I was still in shock over what had happened in the last few hours when the phone rang.

"It's Frieda!" Mom called.

"My project is going to be a disaster." My BFF's words came rushing out. "I can't work with Brianna. As soon as I got home from school, she called my house. She wanted me to come to her place, immediately. I went to *her* house. We chose *her* idea and we're doing it *her* way. It's stupid. I don't even like the animal she picked. It's the monk seal. I've never heard of that seal before. But the worst part is that she doesn't even want to follow Mr. R.'s rules! You know how he always reminds us to reuse, reduce, recycle. But that's not good enough for her. Bossy Brianna is going to buy a fancy new board for our display!" Frieda took a deep breath and sighed loudly.

"Don't forget about upcycle. Did you try to tell her that Mr. R. wants us to — "

Frieda cut me off and continued her rant. "We can only work at *her* house. Her mom and her older sister are just as bossy as she is. They were yelling at each other and at Brianna." Gasping for breath, she continued. "I'm telling you, I'm going to talk to Mr. R. tomorrow and tell him that I need to work with you. You can't work with Cedar, either. He doesn't even talk."

"Yeah . . . About that," I stammered. "Cedar does talk."

"What! When did he talk to you?"

"He came over," I answered. "He's actually nice, and he had a great idea."

I heard her swallow. "So, you won't help me when I talk to Mr. R?"

"Well, I don't know."

"I thought you were my BFF!" Frieda bristled.

"I am! I'm always going to be your BFF!"

"I'll see you tomorrow."

The anger in her voice lingered on the line after she hung up. The knot returned to my stomach and I felt my brow furrow.

"What happened?" Mom asked.

"Frieda's mad that I want to be Cedar's partner for the project. She hung up on me."

"Why don't you call her back after supper?" she suggested. "You know how she gets when she's hungry, maybe food will help her calm down."

"I guess you're right." I sighed. I thought about riding over to see her, which reminded me that I couldn't ride anywhere without alerting the entire neighbourhood. "Oh, Mom, my bike is making that scary noise when I pedal again."

"It probably needs some grease. I'll fix it later."

After supper, it was Mom's turn to do dishes. I printed out information about the northern spotted owl using old flyers with advertising on one side to fulfill Mr. R.'s reuse, reduce, recycle requirement. In my research, I learned that these owls are nocturnal hunters. Flying squirrels, woodrats, mice, birds and insects make up their dinners. Yuck. The more I read about the northern spotted owl, the more excited I became. I had a feeling that, with Cedar's help, it was going to be a good project. Once I had a large pile of information, I went up to my room and gathered all my stuffed owls on my bookshelf. Not one of them looked like the northern spotted owl.

I decided not to call Frieda back. I couldn't think of anything to say to make her feel better because I felt encouraged by what had happened with Cedar and I knew she wouldn't like that. Anyway, I knew Mr. R. wasn't going to let her change partners. He always sticks to his plan, one of his other rules. He's a stubborn man.

Bossy Brianna's remark about "Mr. Birch Tree" talking my ears off still bothered me. Would she still make fun of us when she learned that Cedar and I were talking?

Chapter 4

WHEN I ARRIVED at school the next morning, Frieda stood watching kids on the swings. She ignored me, but I walked up to her anyway.

"Still going to talk to Mr. R?" I asked.

"What's the point if you don't want to work with me?" she answered flatly.

"I'd work with you, but I don't think he is going to let you change partners."

"It doesn't matter anyway. Everybody else, including you, is happy with their partner." Frieda strode off and left me alone by the swings. I felt awful.

When we entered our classroom, Mr. R. was unpacking his backpack and piling books and papers on his desk.

"By now, you must have thought about endangered animals. Maybe you have already discussed and decided which one you will research with your partner." He cleaned off part of the blackboard. *"Together we will make a list, of all species that still exist."*

I looked around the room. Where was Cedar? Was he going to be late? Was he not coming to school at all? Did I scare him off yesterday?

I tried to get Frieda's attention by pointing at our teacher's shirt, which had a leatherback turtle painted on the front, but she looked the other way.

In the computer lab, each team was assigned a computer to research their endangered species. Mr. R. brought in a stack of papers that had been used on one side so we could print responsibly. "Bring used cardboard from home for your background and use only materials that are found," he announced as we fired up our computers. I already had a ton of information on the northern spotted owl in my backpack, but I turned my computer on anyway. I decided to look through our material one more time to make sure we hadn't missed any important information.

"Hey Rebecca! Did your partner stand you up?" Brianna sneered. Of course she would make fun of me for this. "Oh, how sad. Don't have a panic attack now!"

My face burned. How could she make fun of something I couldn't control? I clenched my fists, but before I could say anything, Mr. R. knelt beside her.

"Brianna, that is extremely inappropriate. Please focus on your own project and don't worry about other teams."

"Rebecca isn't even on a team!" she continued.

"You can leave the room if you don't stop now." He crossed his arms.

Brianna rolled her eyes and turned back to her project. She stayed quiet, but Eric smirked at me. I could hear him snickering. Worst of all, though, was Frieda. When I tried to catch her eye, she turned away.

"Where is Cedar?" I whispered when Mr. R. came over to check on my research.

"I don't know. Did he work with you at your home?"

I pointed at my notes.

"I see you two found a fair amount of information. That's awesome." He walked over to the next team.

I agreed. I still felt overwhelmed by how easy it was to work with Cedar, and I wondered why my teacher wasn't surprised. Had he known that we would work well together?

The rest of the day was awful. Every time I tried to talk to Frieda, she walked away. Several times, Brianna pointed at me and giggled. Eric snorted when he looked at me, and Ben chuckled.

"You and Mr. Cedar Bench will have a great project. Especially when he's a no-show!" Brianna jeered at the end of the day.

Last night, I thought our project was going to be fun. Now I hated it.

After school, I pedalled home in a fury. I slammed the front door and threw my backpack on the floor.

"What's wrong?" Mom asked. "Why is my smart daughter so angry?"

I slumped down at the kitchen table and put my head in my hands. Mom made blueberry tea. She had cut apples into stars and peeled oranges into flowers. Her after-school snacks were always more elaborate when she had writer's block — the vampires must have still been stuck.

"How's your BFF?" she asked carefully.

"She wouldn't talk to me. I hate school!"

"You've never hated school before."

"Brianna kept making fun of me, and so did Eric and Ben. And Cedar wasn't even at school. Frieda ignored me all day." I felt like crying. I shoved a big piece of apple into my mouth. By chewing hard, I stopped the tears.

"Think of how frustrated Frieda must feel that she has to work with Brianna. Why don't you go see her?" Mom suggested.

"What am I going to say?"

"You'll think of something." Mom walked over to her desk, where her laptop sat open. "Back to my vampires."

"It's not nighttime yet!" I could tell that she wasn't even thinking about my problems anymore.

"Home by six!" Mom flashed her teeth like a set of fangs.

I grabbed my bike and slowly pedalled over to Frieda's. All the way to her house, I tried to think of what to say.

I rang the doorbell.

Jason, Frieda's second-eldest brother, opened the door. "Hey, owl girl," he teased. "Whoo, whoo are you?"

"I'm having a hootin' time," I answered, flapping my wings. "Is Frieda home?"

"She went to Brianna's to work on their project. Did you and Frieda . . . ? Never mind. None of my business."

Tears streamed down my face as I biked home. Back in my room, I journalled madly about my anger and frustration.

. . .

The phone rang just before supper, but Mom picked it up before I could run downstairs. Was it Frieda, finally ready to talk to me?

"Rebecca! It's Gram!" Mom called up to my room.

I jumped up, threw my journal and pen on the bed and ran into the kitchen. I was a little disappointed that it wasn't Frieda, but Gram always made me feel better.

"Hi Gram," I said when Mom handed me the phone. I took it to my room and closed the door.

"Tell me about your project." Gram sounded interested. She always wanted to hear about my assignments and loved to offer help, even though her help never worked out.

"I hate it." I knew she'd understand. She listened when Mom didn't, and she always took my side. Always. Gram knew everything about school, Frieda and even Bossy Brianna.

"Your mom told me that Brianna is bullying you again, and that Frieda is ignoring you because you two can't be partners." Gram paused. "Frieda will come around. Best friends always make up."

"I hope so. I just don't know how."

"Tell me about Cedar, your partner."

"He never talks in class, and I was really worried. How could we work together if he didn't say anything? But then he came over and it turns out that he can talk, and he's very nice."

"That's amazing." Gram sounded surprised. "And that's why Frieda is mad at you?"

"She has to do the project with Brianna. She hates working with her."

"She should talk to your teacher," my grandmother suggested.

"Yeah, maybe she should." I sighed.

"Why do you call your teacher Mr. R?" she asked.

"Because he reuses, reduces and recycles everything, like *everything*! Instead of three Rs, we just use one. Oh, and there is another R for rhyming."

"But what's his real name?"

I had to think hard. We never used his full name. When it came to me, I rolled my Rs just like he had when he first introduced himself in class. "Rodrigo Raymond Reid. See, Gram? Three Rs. He also speaks mostly in rhyme and wears animal shirts he buys at the thrift shop. And you should see his hair — dreadlocks blown into a nest because he bikes to school. He doesn't even own a car. But I like him. He wants us to help the environment."

"Well, he sounds like an interesting man, but he's giving his students a big responsibility."

I totally agreed with her.

"Does he have a family? How old is he?" Gram asked.

"Yup, his dog, Friendly, is his family. He had his birthday the first week of September. I think he turned thirty-six."

"Were his parents from Jamaica?" Gram always asked so many questions.

"Yeah, I think he said he was eight when he came to Canada."

"Maybe I can help you with your project."

"Thanks, that would be cool." It was nice of her to offer, but I had no idea how she could help. "We're researching the endangered northern spotted owl."

"I'm not good with computers, but if you think of anything I can do, let me know. Right now, I'm cleaning out my basement before I move into the retirement home next month. I found boxes of felt and other craft supplies. Remember when we had a craft group at church? Somehow, I ended up with all the materials when the club discontinued. I thought you could use that stuff at school."

"Thanks, we can definitely use it!"

"Whatever it is, Rebecca, we have no room!" Mom opened my bedroom door holding a pile of folded laundry.

"I'll store it under my bed for now!"

"There is no room under your bed." Mom sounded annoyed.

"I'll take it to school!"

"I'll come over shortly to drop off the boxes," Gram said.

"Thanks, Gram."

"Supper's ready, Rebecca." Mom sighed and left my room.

"I've got to go Gram, suppertime. Love you! See you soon!"

"See you soon, hon."

. . .

Supper was homemade Thai food, one of Mom's specialties. We had just finished eating when Cedar called.

"Hey, did you get to work on the project today?"

"Yes, but where were you?"

"I . . ." he trailed off, then went silent. I worried that the call might have been disconnected, but then I heard him breathing.

"Never mind, forget I asked." I could tell it made him uncomfortable, so I tried to move the conversation along. "Will you be there tomorrow?"

"Yes, and I found more interesting stuff. We can even adopt an endangered animal."

"Can we adopt a northern spotted owl?" I asked. "Will you bring that information to school?"

"I will. But if we want to adopt an owl, we'll need money."

"Could we do a fundraiser? Would Mr. R. agree to that?"

"I don't know. Maybe. Can you come over to my place on Saturday, in the morning? I found materials for our display."

"Sure." I wondered what his house would be like. In my mind I saw the magical wooden eagles standing proudly at the entrance. I would get to see them up close, and I would meet the wolf in his yard.

• • •

After supper, Gram came by in her clunky old Toyota. As always, her glasses were halfway down her nose. She wore a blue and white skirt with a navy knitted cardigan and her favourite straw hat. My grandmother loved long, flowing skirts and she owned many. Not only did she bring two boxes of craft stuff, but she also put a tin of cookies on the table.

While she and Mom discussed vampires and drank ginger tea, I tried the cookies and checked out the treasures. I found felt squares in every colour imaginable and a container with buttons of every shape and size. I discovered a bag with a million different shades of embroidery floss, a bag of pompoms and hundreds of pipe cleaners. I picked up a glass jar filled with wooden beads and little vials of tiny, sparkling glass beads. I wished I knew what to do with all this cool stuff so it wouldn't just sit around and take up space. For now, I took the boxes to my room and stacked them beside my bed.

"Rebecca, what have you learned so far for your project?" Gram patted the chair beside hers.

"Well, the northern spotted owl is really endangered." I sat down and took another cookie. "Did you know that their habitat is threatened by logging and climate change?"

"I believe it. How can you help protect these owls? You can't stop the logging." Gram's interest in the project excited me, and for a moment I forgot about the trouble it was causing between me and Frieda.

"Cedar found information on how to sponsor them."

"You probably need to raise money for that. How will you do it?"

"We don't know yet." Suddenly, I looked at my mother. "Mom, can you write a book about the spotted owl and sell it?"

"I don't think Mr. R. intends for the parents to do the project."

She was right. I knew for sure that he didn't want parents to do the work. "Maybe we can bake owl cookies and sell them. I have the perfect cookie cutters!"

"I can't help you with those, either." Mom shook her head. "My cookies always turn into hockey pucks. I've never mastered the art of baking."

"And don't look at me," Gram added. "Where do you think your mom got her lack of baking skills? You told me that Cedar's grandfather is an artist. Maybe he knows how to bake cookies."

"But you just brought cookies." I pointed at the tin.
"They're from the bakery across the street from me!"
We all laughed. The day didn't turn out so bad after all.

Chapter 5

I WAS RELIEVED about two things the next morning. Cedar biked into the schoolyard, and Frieda waved at me when she put her bicycle away.

Before lunchtime, Mr. R. gave us a bit more time to work with our partner in the computer lab.

"I'll show you what I found on the internet last night." Cedar pulled up the website. "The site is called *Defenders of Wildlife*."

"*Defenders of Wildlife?*" I burst out laughing. "That must be why Mr. R. called us 'wildlife defenders.'"

Cedar chuckled and turned back to the computer. "You

can adopt an animal from one of the endangered species on this list. You'll get adoption papers, a photo and a stuffed animal — except when you adopt the northern spotted owl." He scrolled through all the stuffed animals.

"Why not?" I asked. There was a snowy owl, but not our owl.

"I don't kn— "

"Look at the lovebirds!" Brianna interrupted, pointing at us. "Look at them talk and laugh. A miracle has happened. Our Rebecca has made Mr. Cedar Bough talk!"

I glared at her in disbelief. She really was cruel. My face burned and I couldn't look at Cedar.

"Brianna, sit at my desk. Nobody is interested in your comments." Mr. R. placed a file in front of her. "Sort these forms for me in alphabetical order." He opened the file and waited for Brianna to sit down.

Brianna rolled her eyes.

"You can finish that job now, or after school," he added.

Cedar and I continued to browse the website in silence. My chest hurt. It was hard to hold in my anger toward Brianna. I felt like hurting her back.

After school, Frieda waited for me. "You're having more success with your partner than I'm having with mine."

Relief washed over me and I couldn't help but smile. "She must be awful to work with. I don't know how you do it."

"No kidding. I hate the project and I hate working with her. Mom said I just have to get through this week and next week and then I'll be free from Brianna. It just feels like a very long time 'til next Friday."

"I'm sorry I can't help you, Frieda. I just wish Brianna would stop being so mean and calling Cedar names."

"I know." My friend sighed. "She's so predictable. And I'm sorry I was so angry with you. Did I tell you what she said about my clothes?"

"No." I knew Frieda hated the clothes her nana bought for her. They were always pink, and she hated pink.

"She told me it was time to wear something grown up instead of baby outfits! Can you believe how rude she is?"

"Yes, I can. I'm surprised she hasn't mentioned that I only wear used clothes."

"And she commented on my hair," Frieda added.

"What's wrong with your hair? Does she want you to dye it purple like hers?"

"Even if she did, I wouldn't go for her stupid hairstyle. I bet you her sister does her hair. Jill's hair is dyed jet black or midnight black or whatever." Frieda threw her arms in the air. "After next Friday's presentations, I'll be free, and we should totally ignore her!"

"I agree, but that's easier said than done. We should stand up to her."

"But how? She's so bossy." Frieda rolled her eyes.

I shrugged. It sounded like a good idea when I said it, but I knew I couldn't stand up to Brianna. She always made me feel stupid, like a nobody.

"Let's get together on Saturday," Frieda suggested.

"I'm going to work at Cedar's in the morning, but we can get together in the afternoon. My gram brought me two huge boxes of art supplies. Maybe you can help me figure out what to do with them." I noticed the disappointment on her face. "Don't worry! After next Friday, we'll both be free again."

We high-fived and biked home. I felt happy. Gram was right, as usual. Best friends always make up.

Chapter 6

"MOM! WHAT'S WRONG?"

Mom sat at the kitchen table with her head in her hands and her glasses beside her. When she looked up, her eyes were red and her face and neck were covered in blotches.

"Is something wrong with Gram?" I tried to think of what else could have happened to make my mother so upset.

Mom lowered her hands and placed them on the table. She took a few deep breaths and spun her ring around and around. Her breathing slowed. I sat beside her and held her hands, waiting.

"I don't know how to tell you." She swallowed hard.

Suddenly, my chest felt like someone had cinched a wire

around it. My breathing accelerated. I needed to focus, or I'd end up with another *thunderbolt*. That wouldn't help Mom with whatever she was so upset about.

"Please tell me," I pleaded. When she stayed silent, I rubbed my chest, hoping the pain would subside. "Remember, it's much worse not knowing?"

She nodded, took another deep breath and said, "Our house has been sold."

"What? How? We never had a sign in the yard! Did he tell you he was going to sell?" I couldn't breathe. "I can't believe it. This . . . this is our home. Where will we go?" I cupped my mouth and nose so I wouldn't hyperventilate. The wire around my chest tightened and my stomach knotted.

"Mr. Wong told me five years ago, when I first rented from him, that he might need to sell this house one day." Mom paused. "But nothing happened for five years, so I didn't see this coming."

"No warning, nothing? But he can't do that, can he? It's not fair. Doesn't he know we have no place to go?"

"No warning. Just a phone call this afternoon to let me know."

"Does Gram know?"

Mom shook her head. "I wanted to tell you first. And I've been dreading it. I hate for Gram to worry about us."

"I know, Mom. I know."

She patted my hands. "Oh, Rebecca. I feel so lost. We were doing so well here, much better than before, when I couldn't afford our apartment. This little house is so perfect. I can pay the rent and we hardly ever have to go to the food bank."

I was lost, too. I remembered how hard it was for Mom when she had to ask for food. We were so lucky when we found this cozy little house, with its big, sunny front window, at half the rent we paid before. I thought we would never leave this happy place.

Tears streamed down my cheeks as I tried to imagine what it would be like not to live in this house, our home. No place could be as perfect. On the outside, a flower box ran the length of the window. Every spring, Mom and I filled the box with pink petunias from which hummingbirds filled their bellies. Several pots of lavender lined the short stone path to the blue metal gate. Our kitchen and its pine cupboards were small, but they worked. The two bedrooms had big beams across the high ceilings. I often pretended that I was sleeping in an old castle. Shelves surrounding my bed displayed my owls, my animal and bird books, the drum I had made in grade three and my special treasures like shiny rocks and sea-shells. In the bathroom, a round window above the toilet overlooked the garden. Behind the house stood our garden shed, where we stored our bikes. Mom and I grew vegetables and daisies, her favourite flower, in our tiny yard. It was so, so perfect.

I fell in love with the blue metal gate the day we moved in. It reminded me of a gateway into a magical story. How could we ever leave this house? I felt sad, sick and angry at Mr. Wong, our landlord.

Mom stared out the window. Her lower lip trembled. She was probably thinking about our nice little house, too, about how it wasn't going to be ours for much longer.

I let out a slow, controlled breath, but the pain in my chest persisted. "I know what Gram is going to say to you."

Mom nodded. "Go get a 'real' job!" we said in unison. We both chuckled a little.

Gram didn't agree with Mom being a writer. She wanted my mother to have a regular job so we wouldn't have to worry about money all the time. I thought being a writer was super cool, though. She wasn't famous or anything, but she had three books published and wrote tons of articles for magazines.

"It's not just the money," Mom continued. "There are no rentals available in this area."

I gasped. "I can't change schools, I can't!" More tears spilled from my eyes.

Mom squeezed my hands. "I'm so sorry we have to leave."

"You didn't tell me when," I whispered when I was able to swallow again. I dreaded her response.

"December 31st. We have two and a half months to find a place."

"But why does Mr. Wong have to sell our home?"

"I heard that his bookstore closed. The economy is not doing well right now. Many businesses are struggling to keep their heads above water. I think Mr. Wong has financial problems and needs money. He probably wouldn't sell if he didn't have to."

"That doesn't help us," I sniffed.

"I know." Mom blew her nose and wiped her eyes. "But with time come solutions, as my father always said."

"Two and a half months is not much time for a solution. I wish Grandpa was still around," I said. "He could have helped us with the solution."

"Yeah." Mom stared out the window. "Dad was always in a good mood, fixed everything around the house and mended my toys when I was a kid. His life's motto was, 'There is a solution for everything.'"

"We should remember his words and not give up." I hugged Mom and hoped that those words and remembering Grandpa would cheer her up.

"Yes, we should remember his words." Mom closed her arms around me and kissed my cheek. "And now we have to let Gram know. Why don't you call her and invite her for dessert?"

"Maybe Gram can help. Maybe she has a solution for us." I dialled her number. Gram picked up on the first ring. "Can you come over for dessert?" I asked.

"I'd love to. See you soon," Gram answered.

"Sorry." Mom managed a thin smile as I hung up. "I forgot, but I don't think there is any dessert in the fridge."

I opened the door and scanned the bare shelves. "Nope, you're right."

"We'll make tea." Mom got up from the table. She wiped her eyes, put her glasses on, cleared the counter and stared out the window some more.

"I'm not hungry," I said. My stomach still hurt and just thinking about food made me feel ill.

"I don't need anything either, we'll skip supper." Mom returned to the table and opened her laptop. "Let's look for a place to live."

I sat down beside her and put my head on her shoulder. We checked the rental listings in our area and then the rest of town. There were some apartments available close to the centre, but Mom said the monthly rent for a two-bedroom apartment was too high.

I was glad we couldn't afford to live downtown, so I didn't have to change schools. On the other hand, though, we had to live somewhere.

. . .

Gram's Toyota pulled up in front of our gate. I squeezed Mom's hand and went to let her in.

"You invited me for dessert, so I expect you are celebrating! But what?" Gram asked when she walked into the kitchen. "I brought some ice cream to get this party started."

Mom didn't answer. My lip trembled and Gram's excitement faded to concern.

"We have bad news." Mom put her arms around her mother. "But maybe a bit of ice cream would make us feel better."

Gram had brought my favourite, chocolate pecan. I took three bowls from the shelf and placed them on the table. Gram filled each with a large scoop of ice cream and we dug in. Even though I felt rotten and my stomach hurt, the cool, velvety ice cream soothed my throat and tasted delicious. I was glad my grandmother had come.

"Mr. Wong sold our house. We have to leave by the end of December." Mom looked down into her ice cream.

Gram gasped. "That's terrible news." She shook her head in disbelief.

For a moment, we were all quiet.

"I'll start asking people at church . . . the choir, my yoga group and my book club." She got up and cleared away the bowls. "There must be houses for rent in this area." She rinsed the bowls and spoons and placed them on the drying rack. "I know the city has plans to build low-income rental houses, but there's no timeline for that project. That won't help you. I'll ask around. Too bad my old house is being demolished, so you wouldn't be able to rent it."

"And it's not close to my school," I added.

Gram gave us both a great big bear hug.

"Thanks, Mom." My mother hugged her back.

After Gram left, I watched my mom. She looked so sad and I didn't know how to cheer her up. "That could be a solution. I mean, the low-income rentals."

"Don't get your hopes up, Rebecca. Those houses haven't even been built, and we need a place by January!" She sighed and rubbed her temples. "I wish we could just buy a place."

"Well, when your vampire story becomes a bestseller, we can just buy every house in the neighbourhood!"

"Well, that's always a possibility!" She pinched my cheek and we giggled.

The phone rang. "You get that."

"Hi Frieda," I answered. I didn't mention the house. I knew I would get anxious and start crying.

"You won't believe what just happened," Frieda said. "My nana came after supper with a new pink dress that she wants me to wear for the presentation. But I can't, Rebecca. I'll look like a baby, just like Brianna said. Please help me!"

"I don't know how." I felt awful for her. Her grandmother bought all her clothes. Suddenly, I had an idea. "Tell your nana that our teacher suggested we wear something with an endangered species on it. I'm sure he'd like that, even if he didn't say it."

"That's easy for you. You can wear your owl shirts, but I have nothing with a monk seal on it. Not even a pink one."

"Mom!" I turned away from the phone. "Can we take Frieda to the thrift shop and find her something with a seal on it?"

"Sure," Mom answered. "Not on Saturday. After school would be best for me."

"Mom and I will take you to the thrift shop, if you don't mind riding the bus."

"Of course I don't mind," she replied. "That sounds really nice."

"I'm sure you'll find something. Or . . ." I chuckled. "Maybe Mr. R. has a seal shirt you can borrow."

"That's not funny!" my friend snorted. "But I would love it if you could take me. My mom would never go there. I think she's embarrassed to buy used clothes."

"How about Friday?"

"Perfect. Thanks, Rebecca. You are my best friend forever."

. . .

That night, I couldn't fall asleep. The bad news wouldn't go away. When I finally travelled to the land of dreams, I found myself on a park bench in my sleeping bag. Just like the homeless people who couldn't afford to pay rent. We always saw them sleeping on benches in Centennial Park when we took a shortcut to the library. Would Mom and I end up like that?

Chapter 7

AS I EXPECTED, the thrift shop had a great selection of animal T-shirts.

"This is so cool." Frieda flipped through the hangers. "I hope I can find one with a seal." She held up a shirt with a dolphin on the front.

In the toy section, I found a small stuffed seal. I tucked it in my pocket to surprise my friend later.

Mom helped too, making sure we looked at the correct sizes. It took longer than we thought and in the end, the kids' section had no seal shirt for Frieda. When Mom checked the ladies' sizes though, we were in luck. She held up a huge black T-shirt with long sleeves and the most gorgeous silver-grey seal printed on the front.

"It's beautiful!" my friend exclaimed. "But it's way too big."

"It's an extra-large, but there's a solution for that." Mom winked at me. "I'll alter it, if you'll let me."

"You can do that?" Frieda hugged her.

Mom and I hugged her back and we went to pay. Her shirt was only three dollars.

"That's so cheap." Frieda closed her wallet.

I sneakily paid for the little stuffed animal and then gave it to her.

"You can't afford that!" Frieda cried.

"It was very cheap," I laughed. She hugged the seal to her chest and smiled.

"I can't believe I don't have to wear that stupid pink dress. I had nightmares about that thing." Frieda skipped ahead of us. "I don't even have to lie to Nana because I'm going to tell her that I *think* Mr. R. would really appreciate it if we wore something that was related to our project." She twirled around on the sidewalk. "And Brianna won't humiliate me with her smart remarks, although I'm sure she'll still find something nasty to say about my curly, carroty hair."

"Your hair isn't carroty," I told her. "Your hair is exciting and colourful. Mine is just dull and straight."

"Women pay tons of money for your auburn shade and your beautiful curls," Mom added.

I wanted to tell Frieda about our house, but she was so happy with her shirt that I couldn't bring myself to spoil her mood.

. . .

When I cycled to Cedar's house on Saturday morning, I was greeted by the many carved animals in his yard. Beside the two eagles at the gate was the wolf Frieda had mentioned. It stood next to the path, watching people come and go. I stopped to examine the magnificent creature. Its beady eyes looked at me as if to say, "Save us from extinction." Carved foxes stood on either side of the door. I stroked their heads before I rang the doorbell.

An older man with a long braid opened the door and welcomed me inside. "Good morning. You must be Rebecca. I'm Cedar's grandfather. You can call me Joe."

Joe was taller than I remembered from the time he came to our school. I had to lean my head all the way back to meet his warm brown eyes. He wore a blue checkered shirt and a leather vest decorated with colourful beadwork.

A painting of a black bear and her cub grabbed my attention as I entered the front hall. Paintings of grazing elk, buffalo and an orca decorated the walls going up the stairs.

"Hi Rebecca." Cedar stood in the doorway, hiding his hands behind his back. "Do you like the paintings?" I nodded. "My great-grandfather painted them. My grandfather used to help him, that's where he learned to paint and carve."

I marvelled at the beautiful colours and intricate detail. Every strand of fur on the bear's back was distinct, almost three-dimensional. I wanted to run my fingers through it.

"Here." Cedar handed me a small cardboard box. "Open it."

I blushed. Shyly, I took off the lid. My eyes opened wide and I gasped when I found a small wooden owlet. It was the northern spotted owl. "Oh, it's so beautiful!" A warm feeling hugged me. "Did you carve it?" I stroked the owlet's wooden feathers.

Cedar nodded and laughed. "You were so disappointed when there was no stuffed spotted owl."

"Th — thank you," I stammered. "You are so talented, just like your grandfather and great-grandfather. It's the most special owl of my whole collection."

Cedar smiled and his eyes sparkled. "Come in," he said, waving me inside.

I hung up my jacket. Cedar hurried ahead of me to a large work room at the back of the house.

"This is our studio," he declared when I caught up.

Large wooden beams held up the ceiling. A huge dream-catcher made with beads and feathers filled a round window at the back of the room. Art supplies were set out on a long table. Several carved animal heads perched on chairs and on the windowsill. Sunlight flooded the room through a wall of windows on the long side of the studio, where patio doors opened into the garden. I looked outside and noticed sunflowers, which must have stood proud and tall during the summer months and now gazed toward the autumn leaves on the ground. Chickadees feasted on their seeds. Enormous spruce trees at the edge of their property hid the house and garden from the street. More sculptures and benches lined the path.

"This is a magical place." I couldn't get enough of the view of the garden.

Cedar nodded. "I'll take you outside after we work." He held up a large piece of strawboard. "Grandpa gave me this for our background."

His words brought me back inside. I looked at the square piece of board and agreed that it would make a perfect background.

"I also gathered pieces of bark and small twigs that we can glue on," he continued.

"It'll look like the forest, the habitat of the northern spotted owl. And it's all found materials! That will make Mr. R. very happy. We should put the owl you carved on one of the branches, once they're glued on."

We started sorting. First, we organized pieces of bark by size. They would be tree trunks. Next, we glued them onto the strawboard.

Cedar was totally focused on the job and worked without talking. There was no hint of the usual sadness in his eyes. A rich forest began to take shape as we added branches.

"We could hang the information from the small twigs," I suggested.

"You're good with the computer, right?" Cedar asked.

"Yes, pretty good. My mom can help if we have difficulties.

We could make a PowerPoint presentation with photos and facts and show it to the class on the whiteboard."

"I like that." Cedar spread glue on a piece of bark. "If we want to adopt one of these owls, we need to sell something to raise money."

"I know. Maybe we could sell carved owls?"

"That would take way too long," he laughed.

Suddenly, I remembered Gram's craft boxes. "Felt owls! Gram just gave me a whole bunch of felt, buttons and beads."

"Perfect!" Cedar stopped gluing. "After we finish our background, we'll sew owls and sell them!"

"Will you come to my house after lunch?" I asked. "We'll have all afternoon to work on them."

. . .

The morning flew by, and we worked straight through to lunchtime without taking a break.

"You were going to take me to the garden," I reminded Cedar as I put on my jacket to head home.

"Show Rebecca the tree house we built." Joe was standing in the entrance, holding the door open for me. "You did a great job on the background."

"Thanks for the board," I told him. "I still have the drum you taught us to make in grade three. I'm not very good at playing it, though."

"I'm sure you'll get there with practice," he said with a smile.

I smiled and followed Cedar out into the sun.

We walked along the path to the back of the property. At the end of the path stood a wooden bench carved with birds sitting on branches. I gazed over at the pond, where a carved turtle and a blue heron stood at the water's edge.

"They look so real." I couldn't resist touching the heron's back, half expecting to feel soft feathers.

Cedar led me through an arbour. Rose blossoms struggled to cling to their stems, their brown petals falling in slow-motion onto the path.

The tree house was hidden from view. It sat on a platform, secured to two large branches of a giant maple tree. A rope ladder dangled from the door.

"Would you like to go up?" he asked.

"I'd love to." We clambered up the rungs. He led the way and opened the door. When I stepped inside, I gasped. The tree house was so much larger than it looked from the outside. A wooden bench lined the walls and sunlight filtered through arched windows on three sides. Treasures like small animal carvings stood on shelves between the windows.

"It's like a storybook tree house!" I was in awe. "Do you come here often?"

Cedar smiled. "This is where I do my drawing and sketching, because the light is always different. This is where I get ideas." He looked at me, his eyes serious. "This is my secret hideout."

"I won't tell anybody, I promise."

As I bicycled home, I couldn't help but think about how wrong I had been about Cedar. He wasn't weird at all, he was actually amazing. I was so excited about our project that I almost forgot about our house being sold.

Chapter 8

THE PHONE WAS ringing when I walked in the door. I lifted the receiver to hear Frieda's voice.

"Can you come over after lunch?" she asked.

"Sorry, I can't. We're still working on our project."

"We're not supposed to do all the work at home. Why are you and Cedar working on it all day? You said you would only work with him in the morning."

"We're making felt owls to sell at school so we can adopt a northern spotted owl."

"It sounds like you and Cedar will be the most creative team." Frieda did not sound happy. "Brianna and I will have the crappiest, most boring project."

"Do you want to help us sew owls?" I asked. "We'll need lots!"

She didn't answer.

"Come to my house and help us. Please?" I begged.

"I'll see." She sighed and hung up.

After lunch, I put the felt, buttons, embroidery floss and beads out on the table. Next, I found Mom's sewing basket.

"Do you need a pattern?" my mother asked.

"Northern spotted owlets look like fluffy balls." I showed her the picture. "All I need for a pattern is a circle."

Cedar arrived with two old pillows. "We can use the stuffing to fill the owls, then we don't need to buy new."

"I like that." I grabbed a piece of paper and a pencil. "We need a circle for the body." I took a glass from the cupboard and traced the bottom with a pencil. Folding the paper double, I cut out two patterns. Next, I took a candle holder from the bookshelf and traced around the base to make slightly smaller circles. When I cut them out against the fold, they looked like a pair of glasses. Soon, Cedar and I were cutting felt circles. We used one colour for the body and a different colour for the glasses.

After we had stitched the glasses onto the body, we needed eyes.

"We can use buttons," I suggested.

Cedar sewed two black buttons onto light green felt glasses, which he fastened to a dark grey body.

"Wow, you are good at sewing," I marvelled. He just grinned.

Before we stuffed and closed the bodies, we embroidered our owlets with polka dots, tiny flowers, feathers and leaves. Then we added a beak and talons. Tiny glass beads made the baby owls sparkle and look "spotted."

"How do we sew the two sides together?" I asked.

"The blanket stitch works best."

"The blanket stitch?" I'd never heard of that one.

"I'll show you." He slowly sewed one of the bodies together with embroidery floss, explaining each stitch as he went. "You need to leave an opening for the stuffing."

By the time we had each stitched up one owl, stuffed their bodies and added a string to hang them from the branches on our display, Frieda walked in.

"Those are adorable!" she cried. "Can I make one?"

Mom's sewing machine was set up on her writing desk. She had been working on Frieda's seal shirt, but she came over to admire our masterpieces. "I love them. Can I make one, too?"

"This is starting to look like an owl-making workshop." I smiled at my best friend.

The table was covered in felt. There were buttons everywhere. As the afternoon went on, little owl bodies grew from our busy hands.

"I love your project." Frieda picked up one of the finished felt owls.

"How are the monk seals?" I felt sorry for her.

"Brianna has cut out all the pictures and glued them on." Frieda rolled her eyes. "The only job I'm allowed to do is to print all the information. It's boring, not like your project."

"You should see our board. Cedar's grandfather gave us this piece of strawboard, and we glued on branches and twigs to make it look like a forest."

"By looking at your owls, I can already imagine how interesting your display is going to be." She sighed. "Brianna didn't let me choose anything. I can't wait for the presentations to be over."

"How much will you sell these for?" Mom held up her little owl.

I looked at Cedar.

"How about three dollars? Or do you think that's too much?" he asked.

"No, I think that's fair," I replied. "I hope we can make enough to help a few animals."

"Maybe everybody in our class could make one," Frieda suggested.

"That's a great idea." Cedar stitched a row of shiny beads around an owlet's eyes. "We could make and sell as many as possible, and adopt as many animals as we can afford."

"Do you really think Eric, Jake or Brianna would sew owls for us?" I asked.

"Probably not." Cedar didn't look up from his stitching.

"Why don't you ever speak in class?" Frieda asked Cedar.

He shrugged. "Everyone thinks I'm weird, and some kids say mean things. Call me names. If I keep silent, they don't bother me too much."

My cheeks burned. I looked at Frieda. Her face was red,

too. "I thought you were weird," she admitted softly.

"So did I," I said, ashamed. "But I've changed my mind. Now that I know you, I think you're very smart, and you're such a cool artist. Your house is like an art gallery. The carved animals your grandpa makes are amazing."

I ran upstairs and picked up the little owl Cedar had carved for me. "Look at this." I handed Frieda my treasured owl.

She looked at it and at my partner. "I've changed my mind, too. You are a cool artist."

Mom made us apple cinnamon tea and a plate of crackers, hummus, carrots and grapes. I looked around the table at my friends. Suddenly, a thought struck me: this could be one of the last times I had friends over to this house. The wire around my chest was back and my breathing quickened. Frieda took my hand, concerned, and she and Cedar both stared at me. Great. Now I had to tell them what was going on.

I cleared my throat and swallowed hard. "I . . . I have to tell you something terrible. We have to move."

"You what? But . . . why? Where will you go?" my friend jumped up from her chair.

"Our landlord sold our house. Well, it wasn't our house, of course. But it felt like it was." Tears pricked my eyes.

"That's terrible!" Frieda placed her hands over her mouth. "Where will you go? When will you leave?"

"The end of December," I answered, choked up.

"Oh, no. Will you have to change schools?"

"Probably, because there are no rentals in this area. We looked online, right Mom?" I turned and looked at my mother. She nodded and squeezed my shoulder.

Cedar didn't say anything. His eyes were glued to his felt owlet.

Quietly, we returned to our sewing projects. I tried to focus, but Frieda's sad face kept reminding me that I might soon have to go to a school without her.

We completed six owlets. They were all different colour combinations, with different eye shapes and various spotted markings beaded and embroidered onto their felt bodies.

Mom got up from the sewing machine and held up the extra-large seal shirt that she had altered.

"Try it on," she urged. She had transformed the shirt into a long tunic by taking in the side seams.

Frieda dashed to the bathroom and returned wearing it. Elastic in the cuffs made the three-quarter length sleeves fit Frieda's arms perfectly. She beamed.

"I love it." She planted three kisses on my mom's cheeks. I clapped and Frieda curtsied.

After my friend went home, I made her a navy blue felt seal with mauve flippers. Sparkling silver beads decorated the head and tail.

"I'll put everything away." I pointed at the clock, reminding Cedar of his six o'clock dinnertime.

He looked up. "I lost track," he murmured. "I'll finish this one another time."

"Maybe we can work on them after school next week." I walked him to the front door.

"I — I can't," he stammered. "I'm seeing my dad every day after school next week."

"Your dad?" I was surprised.

"He was released from jail last Tuesday. That's why I wasn't at school." He zipped up his jacket.

I couldn't believe what he had just said. "Where is he now?"

"Downtown, in some place." Cedar grabbed his bike, jumped on and left me standing gobsmacked in the doorway.

"His father was in jail," I told my mother. "I didn't even know he had a father. I wonder where his mother is."

"You never know what others carry with them." Mom's face became serious. "I think Cedar hauls a heavy load. No wonder his eyes are sad." She stared out the window. "I can't imagine the challenges he's facing."

I thought about Mom's words and I felt for Cedar. I was glad his grandfather looked after him. Joe seemed like a very warm person.

"Now that we're getting to know him, do you still think he's weird?" Mom asked.

I felt my cheeks burn and shook my head.

That night, I thought about what Cedar had said about his dad. What would be worse: having no father, like me, or having a father in jail?

Chapter 9

ON SUNDAY MORNING, I cut out more owlets. Mom didn't have time to sew any. She needed to finish articles for two different magazines.

Just before lunch, Cedar called. "Would you and your mom be interested in going to The Raptors? We'll be able to see the owls fly."

"The Raptors?" I asked. "Isn't that the place off the highway where they keep birds of prey?"

"Yeah, it's an education centre where you can learn about birds. They have owls."

I wondered how the owls could fly free without escaping.

I'd heard about The Raptors, but I'd never been. "Do we get to see real owls?"

"Yes, and we'll watch a flying demonstration. It's really cool."

"But we don't have a car." I bit my lip.

"Grandpa said he'll drive us there."

I smiled. "Cool! Just let me ask my mom."

"Sounds like a great idea," she called without looking up from her typing.

"We'll pick you up at four," my new friend said.

"See you at four."

I finished three more baby owls and lined them up. Nine unique felt owlets leaned against the books in the bookcase.

Mom came to admire them with me. "You and Cedar have come up with a great project." She kissed the top of my head. "I'm sure you'll inspire other students to help endangered species."

"You could write an article about our project," I suggested.

"Great idea. I'll think about it."

. . .

At exactly four o'clock, a beat-up blue station wagon pulled up in front of our house. Cedar rang the doorbell just as we put on our jackets. We walked out to the car and Mom introduced herself to Joe, who opened the passenger door for her. As Cedar and I climbed into the back, I inhaled the scent of forest, of pine and spruce trees.

"We just picked up some branches from the woods at the end of our road." Cedar pointed behind him. "We left them in the back."

We drove in silence. Cedar's grandfather turned onto the highway. The Raptors was north of our town, just off the main road.

"I've made an appointment," Joe announced. "The public flying demonstrations are at noon, but I asked for a private demonstration." He pulled up to a building marked, "OFFICE."

"A private demonstration? How luxurious." Mom smiled, but sounded a little worried. "Where do we pay?"

"It's all been taken care of."

"But you're also driving us."

Joe just smiled.

The scent of decomposing leaves hung in the chilly air as we passed through the gate to the visitor centre. As I shivered in my jacket, a man came out to greet us. He and Joe shook hands and he introduced himself as Alex, our guide.

I forgot about the cold as Alex explained how many species of birds of prey were at risk. "The biologists and falconers at the centre want to bring people closer to these magnificent birds. Their goal is to educate the public so they can understand the critical role these birds play in maintaining the ecological balance of our planet."

"We're working on a project about the northern spotted owl," I told Alex.

"We don't have a spotted owl here, but did you know they started a breeding program in Langley, right here in B.C.? You should check out their website. It's fascinating, what scientists are doing to protect these species."

"That's amazing! We'll have to check that out," said Cedar.

We walked past the office building and were welcomed by a chorus of screeches — some more ear-piercing than others. Large cages, each home to a different species, lined the path on both sides.

First, we visited a large enclosure where a bald eagle was perched on a tree stump. Its keen eyes followed us. The bird in the next enclosure looked similar, but was totally brown.

"This is a young bald eagle," Alex explained, gesturing to the brown bird. "The head and tail feathers will turn white as it matures, which could take five to eight years."

"The bald eagle on the left looks exactly like the two you carved," I said to Joe.

He smiled. "I think it's the other way around, Rebecca."

I agreed, but the resemblance between the carved and the real eagle was amazing regardless. We followed Alex to the cages that housed the owls.

A barn owl ogled me with curious eyes as if to say, "Why didn't you pick me for your project?" I instantly fell in love. I read on the information board that barn owls use their strong sense of hearing to hunt small rodents.

The turkey vulture was ugly and made a horrible sound. Alex called it the garbage patrol bird because it cleans up roadkill. Its sharp senses help it detect pieces of raw meat from kilometres away.

"We've got some more owls ahead," called Alex as he led the way.

He introduced us to the barred owl, with its white speckles, and the Eurasian eagle owl, one of the largest owl species in the world. The Eurasian eagle owl was almost wiped out in Europe, but here was one on our very own Vancouver Island, alive and well.

"In Western Europe, breeding programs are highly successful in reintroducing the Eurasian eagle owl in places where there were none left," Alex told us.

I was glad to hear that people in Europe tried to save their endangered species, too.

"Another powerful hunter is the great horned owl," our guide continued. "This bird even eats skunks and porcupines."

"Skunks and porcupines," Cedar repeated. "Wow!"

"Look at this one!" I called when we approached the next cage. "This little owl is wearing glasses."

"It's the spectacled owl." Our guide pointed at the bird's head. "You're right, Rebecca. The white markings around its eyes make it look like it's wearing glasses."

"When will we see them flying?" Cedar asked.

"Very soon. We've arranged for you to see the great horned owl. It will fly free."

I couldn't believe they would just let the birds fly. "Won't they escape? Or fly away and get lost?"

Alex laughed. "Here comes Talia. She's one of our falconers. She'll tell you the secrets of these mysterious and intelligent birds of prey."

Talia, a tall girl with cropped pink hair and a nose ring, wore a long leather glove on her right arm. She explained that the glove was called a "gauntlet." After introductions, she took us back to the cage with the great horned owl.

"You have to remember that most of these birds were born in captivity, and this is their home. Some have been injured and rehabilitated here. This is the place where they get fed." She opened the enclosure and the owl swooped down from a branch onto her arm. "The owl also knows its handlers."

"Wow," I whispered. "This is so cool."

Cedar didn't take his eyes off the majestic bird.

Mom and Joe stood back. I could tell from Mom's face that she was totally fascinated. Her bottom lip was sucked in and her eyes were wide open. That was her "inspiration" face. I knew she would write about these amazing creatures later.

I watched Talia feed the owl small pieces of something I couldn't identify.

"Mice," she said with a smile. "One of its favourite treats."

We were allowed to watch the owl up close. I loved how the feathers, with their soft markings, overlapped each other, protecting the bird with a thick coat. Its piercing eyes kept scanning our group, keeping watch over all of us. I loved how it screeched, softly, as if it was talking.

"We'll walk over to the field behind the building and meet Jim, the other falconer."

We followed Talia. I was amazed at how well the great horned owl stayed on her arm. It could've easily flown away. We didn't speak until we met Jim, who also wore a leather gauntlet on his arm and carried an extra one.

Jim took us to a large, open area. On one side were several rows of wooden benches. The field bordered a wooded area where tall birch, hemlock and spruce trees, low-growing shrubs, huge ferns and other vegetation showed off their fall colours. Several tree stumps of varying heights marked the perimeter of the flying field.

Talia placed a small piece of meat on the nearest stump. The owl lifted off and perched on the stump, snatching up the treat with its sharp beak. It screeched several high screeches as it surveyed the area.

"I'll take him up the path behind the trees." Jim pointed to the right of the large field.

"Jim will let the bird go and it will fly down and land on my arm," Talia explained. "You'll sit on those benches behind me for this demonstration, so you won't confuse the owl."

We settled onto the wooden benches and watched Jim disappear with the bird perched calmly on his arm.

Holding my breath, I watched and waited until the great horned owl emerged from the foliage. On enormous wings it sailed toward us, screeching continuously. When it finally landed on Talia's arm, it pushed its head into a little pouch and found a treat.

"This is magical." I was in awe. The owl looked proud. Its

head swivelled from Talia to us, blinking as if to say, "I know, I am incredible."

Talia lifted her arm and the bird bobbed its head in a little dance before it took off toward Jim.

"Who's next?" She held up the extra gauntlet and looked from Cedar to me.

"You go." I pointed at Cedar.

"Okay." Cedar pushed his hand into the leather glove.

"You hold your arm out like this." She demonstrated by lifting her arm and holding it away from her body. "You need to stand very still. I'll put a treat on your arm, which the owl will smell."

We waited and watched. I could feel the tension radiating from Cedar's body.

Talia raised her arm.

I focused my eyes on the trees, where I knew Jim and the great horned owl were waiting. Suddenly, the giant bird swooped down. It hardly moved its wings as it crossed the field. Several seconds later, it landed smoothly on Cedar's arm. All I'd heard was a soft swoosh and a screech. The way the owl sailed down reminded me of gliders I had seen at the airport. Planes without engines don't make a sound either. I realized the bird needed to fly silently to hunt and was surprised that the screeches didn't alarm its prey.

Cedar's eyes sparkled when he watched the owl snatch the small treat on the gauntlet.

"Raise your arm." Talia motioned to him.

Cedar moved his arm up and the owl lifted off, screeching as it vanished into the trees.

Next, it was my turn to wear the gauntlet.

"Do you remember how to hold out your arm?" Talia watched me put on the leather glove.

"Yes, I remember." My heart thudded with anticipation. I looked at Mom. She smiled at me.

Talia signalled for Jim to release the bird.

I held my breath and stared at the wondrous creature that soared toward me. My eyes stayed glued to the owl as it approached. My arm jolted when it landed. It was so close, so big and heavy. Its soft feathers brushed my face. Quickly, it grabbed its treat and screeched as if to say, "Thank you." Tears filled my eyes. This was the most magical moment of my entire life.

"Move your arm up." Talia pointed at the bird.

I lifted my arm. The bird screeched and hopped onto Talia's arm.

"Did you enjoy that?" she asked.

I nodded and wiped my face on the sleeve of my jacket.

"How long have you been a falconer?" Cedar stepped toward us.

"I've worked here for five years and I've been a falconer for three," Talia answered. "Did you know that our raptors are working birds? We have contracts with airports, landfills and large construction sites."

"I've heard that some birds chase seagulls away from the

airport." Cedar smiled at the owl. "Does this one do that?"

"We have trained falcons, hawks and eagles. The owls are nocturnal and wouldn't be very good during the daytime. The raptors chase away problem birds at worksites. We drive the birds to the site in their cages with their heads covered. Then, when it's time to let them go, we take the covering off."

"They don't escape once they're free? How long is the training?" I asked.

"It depends on how quickly the birds catch on and get used to the noise of the engines. And yes, they always return, because they know where their treats are kept."

"We need to come back for another visit." Joe had joined us. "There is still so much to learn about these amazing birds."

"Come during the summer months, when we offer educational programs."

"Could we volunteer?" I asked. I knew Mom didn't have money to pay for such a program.

"You're still too young to volunteer." Talia smiled at me. She led us back to the cages, where the great horned owl returned to its tree in the enclosure. Before it settled on its perch, it screeched.

"I'm so glad you let us watch the flying demonstration," I told Alex when he joined us.

He winked at Joe. "This session was a special request. We are thrilled when young people show an interest in our program and want to take action."

I looked back at the great horned owl. It watched us from its branch as we left The Raptors. Before we closed the doors of the station wagon, I heard its screech cut through the air one more time.

Chapter 10

"THANKS FOR TAKING us, Joe," I said while I settled into the backseat. "I didn't know they would do a special event just for us. I loved seeing all the birds of prey, but the owls are my favourite."

"I've volunteered with the centre in the past. I was so impressed with your project that I called Alex and asked if you two could see the owls fly."

Cedar was quiet on the way home. He stared out the window.

"You must be glad your dad is out of jail," I said, trying to break the silence. He didn't respond, just stared at his hands.

"I'm sorry. It's none of my business." I felt silly for asking him and making him uncomfortable. I turned away and looked at the city lights.

"My father has a lot of problems," he said after a while. "He's an alcoholic and uses drugs. That's why my mom left with my two sisters."

Surprised by his revelations, I felt sad for him. So he did have a mom, and sisters. I had so many questions but I was afraid to ask.

Mom invited Cedar and his grandfather for tea, but Joe said they needed to get home.

"Thanks for the magical afternoon," I said to Joe. Now that an owl had landed on my arm, I loved them even more and I promised myself I would do my bit to protect them.

Inside, I told Mom what Cedar had said about his father, his mom and his sisters.

"Maybe needing to move isn't as bad as what Cedar is going through." She hung up her jacket.

"And maybe not having a father is better than having one in jail," I added cautiously.

"Rebecca, not now!" Mom said crossly, clenching her teeth.

"If not now, then when?" I asked, but she ignored me. I agreed that Cedar's issues seemed much worse than mine, but not knowing who or where my father was and not having a place to live were serious problems, too.

· · ·

On Monday, I told Frieda about our afternoon at The Raptors with Cedar and his grandfather.

"Those two are so cool." Frieda placed her bike in the rack beside mine.

"Why did we ever think that Cedar was weird?" I asked.

"Because he didn't talk and he dressed differently. But so do I, in my pink baby outfits. And you're weird too, when you have a panic attack."

"Or wear used clothes," I added.

"Your clothes don't look weird or used at all." Frieda pointed at my hummingbird hoodie. "You always look nice, and your clothes are classy."

"But I'm sure Brianna finds my outfits weird. And you're right. Everybody has their own weirdness."

"How many owls did you make?" Frieda asked.

"We have nine so far. Will you help me make more this week?"

"I can help you today. My nana is moving to my Aunt Rachel's place. Mom and I are going to help her pack every day after school, starting tomorrow. Oh, and by the way, Mom liked the seal shirt! She says I'm allowed to buy my own clothes at the thrift shop once in a while. I have to stand up to Nana and tell her to stop buying my outfits."

"Way to go, Frieda!" I high-fived her.

. . .

Cedar had hardly spoken to me at school that day. His eyes seemed even sadder than usual. I imagined that he was worried about his dad.

"Is Cedar not helping to sew more owls?" Frieda asked as we biked home after school.

"He had an appointment, I think." I didn't want to tell her what Cedar had told me. It seemed hard for him to talk about it, and I didn't want to betray his trust.

We finished one owlet each. Frieda's was purple and white. Mine was green with blue glasses and pink button eyes.

On Thursday, the last day before our presentations, Mr. R. gave us some more time to work with our partner. Cedar drew an amazing northern spotted owl, which I coloured and cut out for our display. Next, we traced the letters for our title and painted them bright orange.

"I'll come over to your house to help organize the pictures and information on your mom's laptop," he said at the end of the day. He pulled his bike from the rack.

"You don't have to if you're busy." I wondered if he was supposed to see his dad.

"I'm free," he answered, looking away.

"Okay, perfect. I bet we could finish in no time." I smiled at him, and he gave me a small smile back. We hopped on our bikes and headed to my house.

"Could we use your laptop one more time?" I asked Mom when we arrived. "This is the last time, I promise."

We printed the information and pasted it on cardboard

squares so it could hang from the branches. Next, we created a file on the computer and organized owl pictures for our presentation.

"Let's check out that breeding facility," Cedar suggested.

We looked it up and found the Northern Spotted Owl Breeding Facility in Langley. According to the website, half of the thirty northern spotted owls left in British Columbia lived there.

"Look, you can adopt an egg!" I pointed at the screen. "Oh, that program only runs in the spring."

"That makes sense. There wouldn't be any eggs this time of year." Cedar kept scrolling. "But you can sponsor an adult northern spotted owl! You will receive a certificate, a photo and a plush owl," he read. "Now you can get one, if we make lots of felt owls and sell them."

"That's really expensive, though." I scanned the list of sponsorship prices, disappointed. "The eggs are much cheaper. I'd rather use the money to adopt a lot of eggs than to get a stuffed owl."

"I think our felt owls are much nicer," Cedar decided.

"I can't find a USB stick." Mom was rummaging through the drawers in her desk. "I'm sure I have one somewhere."

"Would you have one at home?" I asked Cedar.

He shook his head.

"How is your dad?" The question had been burning on my lips all afternoon.

Cedar stared at the screen as if it would give him an answer.

"He wants me to live with him," he said softly.

"Where? Downtown?" I didn't want to think about Cedar leaving now that we had become friends. "Do you want to live with your dad?"

He shook his head.

"What about your mom? Can you live with her?"

Again, he shook his head. "My mom has a boyfriend, and my sisters are half sisters. I only see them during school holidays. They live on the mainland."

Wow. I couldn't believe how complicated his life was.

"Where is your dad?" Cedar asked, without looking up from the screen.

My face grew hot. I looked over at Mom, who was searching through papers in a file at her desk. She didn't seem to have heard the question.

"I . . . My dad's in Australia, I think. He doesn't know about me. I don't know him." I swallowed hard. This was not information I liked to share. Only Frieda knew, and she'd promised never to tell anybody.

Cedar looked up from the screen. His sad eyes met mine.

"That's hard," he said softly. "Don't you ever wonder what he looks like?"

"Yes," I whispered. I often wondered who my dad was. If he was really in Australia, whether he had a family, why my mom didn't want him to know that he had a daughter. Every time I asked her she either avoided the question, changed the subject or told me that she would give me the answer when I was older.

"Do you like living with your grandfather?" I asked.

"Yeah. My grandpa is lonely without my grandma and we do a lot of cool things together."

"When did you start living with your grandparents?"

"Five years ago, when my mom moved away and my dad was in jail."

"Was your dad in jail for the whole five years?"

Again, Cedar shook his head. "He's been in and out of jail. I need to go." He stood up. His jaw was clenched, like he was holding back tears. "Do we have everything for tomorrow?"

"I'll bring the pictures if Mom can find the USB stick," I replied. I packed the finished owlets and the felt, beads, buttons and stuffing in a box to bring to school. "When should we ask Mr. R. if we can sew owlets during class time?"

"First thing. I'll bring the background."

"How are you going to carry it on your bike?"

"Grandpa is driving me. We'll pick you up."

"Thanks. Mom, did you hear? Joe's driving me to school tomorrow, you don't have to come with me."

"Great." Mom was now flipping through folders in her filing cabinet.

"Did you find the stick?"

"Uh-uh." She shook her head. "But I will. It has to be here somewhere. There's some stuff on that stick that I need."

"Good luck finding it." Cedar put on his jacket. "See you tomorrow."

Chapter 11

"DON'T LOSE IT." Mom pulled the USB stick out of her laptop. Late last night, she remembered that she had put it in a special place. We quickly copied our presentation onto the stick after breakfast.

"Can you save your pictures on the laptop, just in case?"

"I don't have time, so please look after it."

"I will." I put the stick in the little pocket of my backpack and zipped it up.

"Where are the little felt owls?" Mom asked.

I pointed at the bag just as a car horn honked.

While Mom picked up the box of felt, buttons and beads, I slipped on my jacket and grabbed the bag.

"Good luck! I'll be thinking of you." Mom blew me a kiss.

Cedar took the box from my mother and placed it in the back of the car. My backpack and the bag of owlets sat beside me on the backseat. I wore my snowy owl shirt and Cedar's sweater bore a great horned owl. Five minutes later, we were at school. It was a much quicker drive than a bike ride.

"Thanks for taking us to school." I opened the back door of the station wagon.

Joe smiled and helped carry our background inside. It looked like we were bringing in a piece of the forest.

"See what I did last night?" Cedar pointed at short pieces of dowel sticking out of the tree trunks. "To hang our felt owls."

Mr. R. jumped up and down when he saw our background. He wore a T-shirt with a blue whale on the front. "I'm so excited for these presentations. You're welcome to stay, Joe."

"I'd love to. The kids have worked so hard." He pointed at our display. "Unfortunately, I have a meeting this morning."

I told my teacher about our plan to have the whole class make felt owls as a fundraiser.

"Yes, of course. We can start making owls in art class this afternoon." I could tell from his grin that he liked the idea.

"And can we use your laptop to show our PowerPoint presentation?"

"I will set that up for you, then you'll know just what to do." He pulled his laptop out of his backpack.

More students arrived before the first bell. The tables that had been set up along the wall were soon filled with displays.

Joe placed our board at the end of the last table. "Good luck, you two." He patted Cedar's shoulder and winked at me.

It took a while for all the teams to organize their projects. Most students had painted their recycled cardboard or covered it with used wrapping paper. Our forest scene was the exception.

Brianna came in last with her brand-new board display. Pictures of the monk seal were glued at the top and Frieda's printed info was at the bottom.

Frieda rolled her eyes. "I'm going to ignore her from now on."

"I will, too. I don't care what Bossy Brianna says."

Cedar and I hung the felt owls on the pegs and I placed the USB stick on top of Mr. R.'s laptop.

"Your owls are adorable." Violet and Karen came over to admire our display. Other students pointed and made comments.

"Those two are after brownie points," Eric snickered, nudging Ben. Jake joined his buddies and made kissing noises at us.

Finally, it was time for the teams to present.

"*I can't wait for what you have to say,*" Mr. R. rhymed. "*I like the info on everyone's display.*"

Before the presentations started, I handed Frieda the little felt seal that I'd made for her.

"Thanks. It's adorable. Now I have two." She gave me a hug. "They're the beginning of my seal collection."

"Your shirt looks great." I hugged her back.

She smiled her biggest smile and her freckles shimmered. She walked over to their display. "We'd like to go first," she announced. "Brianna, let's get this over with!"

"We should go last!" Brianna stuck out her chin. "And by the way, why are you wearing that stupid shirt? I thought you would wear something pink on this special occasion," she sneered.

But Brianna's insults couldn't erase the smile on my friend's face. She pointed proudly at the seal on her tunic.

Mr. R. walked over to their display. *"Brianna, it's time for the two of you to share. Show us how much you and Frieda care."*

"But . . . I . . . We . . ."

It was the first time I'd ever seen Brianna stumble. She quickly recovered, though, and walked over to Frieda. With her arms crossed, she said, "It was your idea to go first, so you can present the monk seal."

I gave Frieda a thumbs up. She pulled her hands from behind her back and revealed her two stuffies.

I clapped. To everybody's surprise, Cedar joined me. Soon, the whole class applauded. Brianna scowled.

While my BFF explained why the monk seal was endangered, Brianna looked the other way. Monk seals were victims of entanglement in the ocean's plastic and debris.

"There are fewer than 1400 monk seals left," Frieda announced. "Last night, I ordered a bracelet made from one pound of trash removed from the ocean to help monk seals recover. I'll share the website with the class." She did the whole presentation by herself while Brianna sulked.

From the other presentations, we learned about the endangered orangutan in Indonesia, the snow leopard, the mountain gorilla, the arctic fox, the orca and many more.

Karen and Violet talked about the sea turtle. They took turns explaining how people in Indonesia collected turtle eggs and sold them. As a result, not many eggs hatched. They both wanted to sponsor a project that helped protect the eggs from poachers while educating the public on the importance of these turtles' survival. The project was called Hannah's Reef, named after Hannah Bywater, who at the age of six started to save money to protect the turtles.

We all applauded.

"I've seen you work together so well! You've become good friends, I can tell." Mr. R. gave them a thumbs up. The girls smiled and giggled.

"Rebecca and Cedar have asked to go last." He walked over to his laptop and turned on the computer. *"I'm sure their presentation will be a blast.* Rebecca, where did you put the stick?"

"On top of your laptop." I ran over to his desk. "Right here." But it wasn't there. I looked beside it. Did it slide onto the floor when Mr. R. opened his computer? I crawled underneath the desk. No stick.

Once more, I looked on top of the desk. I lifted up the laptop, moved books and papers. No USB stick. "I know for sure I put it there. I can't lose it. My mom needs it back."

Cedar started looking. Soon, everyone was looking. The stick was nowhere to be found. It didn't make sense. It had to be here somewhere. The wire tightened around my chest and I struggled to breathe. My stomach twisted into a nasty knot. Another *thunderbolt* had struck.

I slid down onto the floor and leaned against the wall. Not now! Not now! I needed to focus. Focus on my breathing, but also on visualizing . . . visualizing what? And then I closed my eyes and the great horned owl came swooping down on silent wings.

Cedar sat down beside me. "Are you having a . . . ?"

"Yes," I wheezed.

Frieda sat down on the other side. "Breathe, Rebecca."

I tried, but my chest was too tight. I felt like I was choking. I closed my eyes and tried again to envision the great horned owl landing on my arm. My breathing slowed as I remembered that magical moment. I could feel its weight and see its soft feathers, piercing eyes and huge talons. I tried to listen to its screeches, but —

"Look, everybody!" Brianna yelled. "Look at poor Rebecca, she's having another panic attack. How convenient!"

"Brianna!" Mr. R. motioned for her to come to his desk.

She ignored him and sneered. "And Mr. Cedar Tree is comforting her. How sweet!"

Cedar got up from the floor. He walked toward Brianna.

Everyone froze. Even I froze, forgetting my predicament. Brianna backed away, looking puzzled. We all waited. You could hear a pin drop.

He stopped in front of her. "Are you jealous?" he asked quietly.

Brianna looked at Cedar, looked at the class, turned around and ran out of the room. Eric started to clap, but Mr. R. motioned for him to stop. Cedar walked away, looking uncomfortable.

Frieda rubbed my shoulders and I began to feel better. My chest still hurt, but I slowly got up and went to Cedar. "Thank you."

"It's okay." He averted his eyes. "But we still haven't found your mom's stick. I have my suspicions, but don't say anything."

"Do you think she — "

He placed his index finger on his lips.

"Alright students, please look around, this USB stick needs to be found." Our teacher came over to me. "Do you need to eat something? Or maybe drink some water?"

"No. Thanks. My stomach doesn't want anything right now."

Mr. R.'s eyes were filled with concern. He clasped his hands together as if he was looking for a solution to my panic problem. But I knew I had to manage this condition myself. A therapist gave me some tools about a year ago, but I still couldn't seem to get them under control. I knew Mom didn't have the money to pay for more therapy right now, so it was up to me.

"Sit down." He grabbed a chair. "Take as much time as you need to feel better."

Frieda checked the ledges underneath the blackboard. Cedar checked the desk again. Everybody checked and rechecked the entire classroom. No stick.

Chapter 12

"*THAT STICK CANNOT DISAPPEAR!*" Mr. R. threw up his arms. "*It must be somewhere around here!*"

The door opened and Brianna entered the classroom. Her face was all blotchy. It looked to me as if she'd been crying. For a very short moment, I felt sorry for her. Nobody in the entire class liked her. But if Cedar was right and she had taken the stick, how could I get it back?

Brianna surveyed the room. All eyes were on her. "Too bad for the lovebirds," she blurted. "They wanted to impress us all."

No one reacted. Even our teacher was waiting for what would happen next.

I looked at Bossy Brianna, who'd bullied Frieda, made fun of my panic attacks and called Cedar names and us love-birds. Suddenly, I stood up and took one step toward her.

"You're jealous of how we've become friends." I looked from Brianna to my classmates. "Once you get to know Cedar, you'll find out how cool he is."

The class stayed silent, but I continued. I felt strong de-spite the pain in my chest. "Nobody ever talks back to you, Brianna. Everybody is afraid of you."

"Why?" She pouted.

"You're bossy. You're never kind. You only say mean things and that's why you have no friends."

Brianna sucked in her lip and looked at Mr. R.

"Rebecca gave you something to think about." He looked at her, but his eyes were kind. *"Reconsider what you've done and don't pout."*

Brianna was speechless. She just stood there. Now that she wasn't in charge, she looked lost. Then, she slowly put her hand in her pocket and pulled out . . . the stick. She threw it on our teacher's desk.

"Here's your stupid stick, Miss Rebecca-So-Smart, Rebecca-Knows-it-All! But you don't know anything! You don't know anything about me!"

Again, the room went silent.

Mr. R. sighed. "You're right, Brianna. We don't know you. We only know an angry Brianna, one who lashes out at her classmates and says mean things. We all know that you have another side. The Brianna who is a kind person, who doesn't want to be mean. Now, take a seat and watch the last presentation."

Brianna sat down.

"Well then, let's proceed. Rebecca? Do you feel better? After all the interruptions, are you and Cedar ready to present?"

Before I could say anything, Cedar grabbed my hand. "Let's do this."

"Wait." I walked over to my backpack and took out the little owl Cedar had carved. Before we started our presentation, I showed my precious gift to the class.

"Cedar is an amazing artist. He carved this spotted owlet for me." I placed the baby owl on one of the branches and let it lean against the trunk.

We took turns explaining why the northern spotted owl was endangered. We showed the PowerPoint presentation of the species and their habitat on the whiteboard. Some students oohed and aahed when they saw how fluffy the owlets were. At the end of our presentation, Cedar showed the class the websites with information on adopting an endangered species and the breeding facility.

"If we raise enough money, we can all sponsor one of these endangered creatures. Actually, there are websites where most of the species we presented on today can be sponsored. On some sites you can receive a certificate, a photograph and a stuffed animal," he added.

"At first, we couldn't find a stuffed northern spotted owl, so we decided to make them for our fundraiser." I pointed to the felt owls on our display. "Then, when we looked at the breeding site in Langley, we found out that we could adopt an egg or sponsor a spotted owl. The egg adoption program is only available in the spring, when the owls lay their eggs. And the sponsorships are expensive. That's why we'd like you to help us by making these little owls during art this afternoon."

Everyone turned to Mr. R. "Please! Please! Please!"

"Yes! Yes!" Our teacher covered his ears. "I have already told Rebecca and Cedar that any student who's interested has the opportunity to sew one of these owlets."

The presentations had taken all morning and we'd learned about twelve endangered species. During lunch hour, everyone talked about the projects, especially about our baby owls. I was glad and surprised to see that Cedar wasn't sitting by himself. Eric, Ben, Jake and Ahmed sat at his table, and he was laughing.

That afternoon, Cedar, Frieda and I taught everyone how to trace the patterns, use the buttons and beads and stitch felt owlets.

Mr. R. used orange and blue felt. "You need to teach me the blanket stitch, Cedar. I know how to sew on buttons and beads, but I don't know that stitch."

Even Jake showed an interest in sewing. Eric said it was girl stuff, but our teacher quickly corrected him.

"It's called survival skills, Eric, and there are no skills that are just for boys or just for girls. You should know that."

Eric's face turned red. "Ouch!" he cried suddenly as he pricked his finger. He ran to the sink, pretending to wash off the blood. The tension was broken and everybody laughed.

The only one who didn't participate and who didn't have fun was Brianna. She sat with her back to the class.

Most owlets were completed before home time. I clapped when I saw how colourful they were, all decorated with beads and intricate stitches.

When class was dismissed, I walked over to Brianna and gave her my owlet. "Here," I said. "You can keep it."

She took the soft baby owl and looked up at me.

"Sorry," she whispered.

I smiled at her.

. . .

The next day, Cedar and I painted a large poster.

BABY OWLS FOR SALE
$3 EACH
FRIDAY AT NOON IN
MR. R.'S GRADE FIVE CLASSROOM
BUY AN OWL AND HELP US
ADOPT ENDANGERED SPECIES!

Everyone helped make and distribute posters to all the classrooms and the office.

During music class, we composed a rap with the help of our music teacher, Mrs. Davies.

"The first thing we need to do is create a beat," she explained. "Then we'll brainstorm lines that rhyme. I'll type them and they'll appear on the whiteboard up here." She turned on her laptop and smiled at the class. "This should be easy for you. You're exposed to a rhyming homeroom teacher every day."

After many tries, we came up with a song:

Extinct, extinct, extinct!
Too many species are extinct!
No more, no more, no more delay
We need to act right now, today!

Don't wait, don't wait, don't wait!
Or it will be too late
For Owl, Turtle, Seal and Whale
Dolphin, Rhino, Wolf and Quail

Grade five students make it clear
These species cannot disappear
They'll adopt to show they care
For endangered creatures everywhere!

We practiced the rap using our homemade percussion instruments — metal cans decorated with bottle caps in different colours.

For the last hour of every day that week we worked on our felt owlets, trying to make as many as possible.

Violet brought in two pillows for stuffing. Ahmed donated

containers with thousands of sparkling beads, and Karen contributed a bag of lace from her grandmother's sewing chest. Brianna worked hard, to everyone's surprise. Her owls shimmered with amazing bead patterns.

"I didn't know sewing owls was this easy," Mr. R. started to rhyme before he stabbed his finger. A drop of blood dripped onto his desk.

"Without the blood, it's easy-peasy!" Frieda finished. We all laughed.

Every morning, Cedar and I made an announcement to encourage everyone in the school to buy our felt owlets. After school, the three of us got together to make more. Even Mom found time in her busy writing schedule to sew a few. By the end of the week, we had 120 owls ready to be sold.

That Friday at lunchtime, every student in the school came to our classroom to buy a baby owl. We were sold out within half an hour. Many disappointed students asked if we had a waiting list. Not only were the students and teachers sad that we were sold out, but our principal, Mrs. Kahn, and our two janitors had hoped to buy felt owlets, too.

Mr. R. wiped his eyes. *"Mother Earth is so lucky to have you, because you know just what to do! The future looks bright for the species you'll save. I admire the responsible way you behave!"*

During recess, we counted the money. We had made $360, enough money to sponsor several species through different organizations.

"What about the people on the waiting list?" I asked when we were back in class.

"We should make more," Brianna suggested.

"We should have another sale." Eric was already at the craft table.

Everybody started voicing their suggestions and ideas until the noise level rose so high that I had to cover my ears.

"Calm down my friends," Mr. R. sang. "Let's brainstorm, and I'll write your ideas on the board, but please: *one idea at a time, or I won't be able to rhyme.*"

"He's crazy," Frieda chuckled.

"Crazy, but nice," I added.

In the end, we all agreed. We needed more felt owls so we could have another sale. The people on the waiting list would get their owls first. Our teacher suggested that we start again after Halloween so we would have time for the special activities he had planned.

"But," he announced, "if anyone wants to sew owlets at home, you can trace the patterns and take the materials you need from the box. We have enough felt, buttons, beads, lace and embroidery floss left over."

Cedar was the first one to put materials in his backpack. Mr. R. was next. I was impressed with my teacher because everybody followed his example. A warm feeling hugged me. I felt so happy to be in this class.

Chapter 13

"CEDAR, WAIT!" I called when we left school.

He turned his bike around as I ran toward him. "How is . . . I mean, are you still going to live with your dad?"

I didn't expect an answer, but he spoke after a long pause.

"I'm moving next weekend."

"After Halloween?"

"Yep."

"But what about school?"

"I don't know. I'm sure there's a school near where my dad lives."

"We'll miss you," I said softly.

He looked away.

The silence lingered until he turned his bike around and left. I just stood there, watching him go. The warm feeling that had hugged me in class this afternoon vanished, leaving me to shiver.

"What's wrong?" Frieda asked, walking toward me. "You look sad."

"I am. Cedar is moving."

"Oh. Did this happen suddenly?"

"Yes."

"Where is his grandfather moving?"

"His grandfather isn't moving. Just Cedar is, but I think Joe will be lonely without him."

"So where is Cedar moving?" My BFF sounded impatient, for good reason. I was dragging this out because I didn't want to mention that Cedar's dad had just left jail.

"Cedar is going to live with his dad. I didn't even know he had a dad, or parents. His mom lives on the mainland and his father lives downtown."

"Oh, that's weird. I mean, that he didn't live with his dad before." Frieda shook her head.

"I know." I mounted my bike and we started pedalling home. "You never know what others go through."

"Like Brianna, who's bullied by her sister and her mother." Frieda looked sad. "When we worked at her house, they were all yelling at each other."

"What were they yelling about?"

"Her mom yelled at Jill that it was her turn to clean out the fridge. Jill yelled at Brianna that she never helps and always makes up excuses." Frieda sped ahead and I followed her. She braked and we stopped at her turnoff.

"And then Jill called Brianna stupid, and Brianna cried."

"And you were there, the whole time?"

"Yep. It was awful. I wanted to run home, but Brianna made me stay to work on the project."

"She gets bullied at home, so she bullies us at school."

"I don't think she has a nice life." Frieda mounted her bike and turned onto her street.

"Everybody's life is so complicated," I called after her. "See you tomorrow." I waved and cycled home.

. . .

"Hey, Mom. Here is your USB stick. I didn't lose it." I walked into the kitchen and placed the stick on her desk. I would tell her about the lost stick and Brianna's outburst later. "Did you finish that article on composting?"

Mom got up from her desk and stretched. "Almost. How was the owl sale?"

"We made enough money to adopt lots of animals! And there's a waiting list for the next round of owlets."

"That's fantastic news. Are you going to make more?"

"Mr. R. said we could make them at home if we wanted to and everybody in my class, including our teacher, took felt and a pattern home. Even Cedar, but he's moving to his dad's next weekend."

"I'm so sorry to hear that." Mom put a mug of hot chocolate in front of me and sat down. "Maybe you can invite him over sometime."

"Besides making owls, what would we do?" I couldn't see us doing things together. He was a boy. It wasn't like hanging out with Frieda. We just talked, listened to music, biked and hiked the trails behind the school. Cedar had spoken to me when we worked on the project, but now that the presentations were over, he didn't really talk to me anymore. I wondered how hard it would be for him to make friends at his new school. When the kids made fun of his name, would he shut down?

I sighed and slurped my drink. "Have you looked at rentals today?"

"There's nothing, Rebecca." Mom stared at her mug. "I look every day."

"Did Gram talk to everyone she was supposed to talk to at her church and stuff?"

"She would have called us." Mom sighed. "Okay, we're not going to worry about the house until after Halloween. What are Mr. R.'s plans?"

"We'll find out on Monday. He'll need all weekend to make up Halloween rhymes."

"That's right." Mom smiled. "I'm sure he'll have some interesting ideas."

"And they will all involve reducing, reusing and recycling."

· · ·

Frieda called right after supper. "Are you coming with me to the thrift shop? My mom suggested we look there for costumes instead of buying new ones."

"What happened to your mom?"

"Right? She used to be too embarrassed to buy secondhand stuff, but now she realizes that it's good for the environment."

"I think our teacher's ideas are rubbing off on everybody," I added.

"She'll drive us this time," my friend said before she hung up.

Mom opened her wallet and handed me a few bills. "I only have $15. I had hoped my cheque for the articles would have arrived by now."

"I don't need to buy a costume." I handed back the money. "I can make something out of our old clothes."

Mom put her arms around me. "I wish things were different," she whispered into my neck. "Maybe I should look for a real job. Gram is right. We can't live on my dreams."

"I want you to stick with your writing. It's so cool." I squeezed her arms and looked into her eyes.

"My writing doesn't put food on the table or pay the bills." Mom turned away. Outside, a car horn honked. "Take the money," Mom urged. "You don't have to spend it."

I hugged her and ran out to the car. Frieda sat in front and I climbed into the back for the short ride.

Her mom let us out at the store. "I'll pick you girls up in about an hour."

The store was packed. With one week left until Halloween, everybody was looking for costumes. As my friend pushed through the aisles, I followed at a distance. The noise level was horrendous, so I was more focused on my breathing than shopping.

"Look at this!" Frieda held up a shell made of green velvet. "I'm going to be a turtle," she declared. "No more pink princess dresses for me."

"You should bring your princess costumes and pink dresses here," I suggested.

I was glad she'd decided on her costume quickly because all I wanted was to get out of the chaos. When I saw the long lineups at the checkouts, I couldn't breathe. My *thunderbolt* had followed me to the thrift shop.

"I'll wait outside," I mouthed, pointing to the exit. I stumbled around adults and children and almost lost my balance before I finally reached the door. Once outside, I leaned against the wall. As I tried to catch my breath, I got mad. Why couldn't I control my *thunderbolts*? What could I do to change or prevent the attacks from happening?

At last, I saw Frieda coming out of the store and waved at her. As soon as she saw me, she apologized. "I'm so sorry. I never thought it was going to be so noisy in there." Proudly, she showed me her purchase.

"You couldn't know. I was trying to think about what I could do to prevent these attacks. I don't know if it would work for me, but can I ask you a favour?"

"Sure."

"If I give you some money, could you buy me earplugs? They would block some of the noise. I could use them in class when everybody goes crazy."

"Yes!" Frieda took the money and ran back inside the store. I sat on the sidewalk, leaning against the wall and holding her turtle shell. The line of men, women and children exiting the store laden with bags and packages seemed endless. I waited and watched the crowds. My breathing slowed and I felt much better.

Finally, my BFF appeared with a big smile on her face. "They were only fifty cents, and it's my gift to you." She pulled me up and handed me the money and the earplugs.

"Thanks. I just hope they work."

"Put them in your ears and let's go back in the store." She pulled me toward the entrance.

As soon as I put them in, I felt like my brain was going to explode. Plugging my ears made the pressure build up in my head. I didn't like the feeling. I would need to get used to wearing them. The street noise was muffled, though, which was a major improvement.

"You should buy earbuds," Frieda suggested. "You can plug them into an iPod. The music would distract you."

"Then I wouldn't hear what was going on. No, these will be okay." I followed her back into the building. I could still hear the noise, but it wasn't as high pitched.

As we left the store for the second time, Frieda's mom

pulled up along the curb. I opened the door to the backseat and we both hopped in.

"I got a great costume, Mom." She held up her green turtle shell.

"Nothing pink?" her mom asked with a smile.

"I'm done with pink, and I need Nana to listen to me."

After they dropped me off, Mom and I went through her closet to see what I could wear for Halloween.

"Nothing," I said, flipping through the hangers one more time. "You don't even own a vampire costume."

"I need to make one, but right now I can't buy fabric. You know what I do have? I still have that green curtain Gram gave us that we never used."

"I can make a cape, put a felt owl on the back and become Super Owl Woman! Or it could say, 'OWL POWER!'"

"I love your idea!" Mom took a chair from the kitchen, climbed up and looked on the top shelf of her closet. She pulled out the green curtain and laid it on her bed.

"It's big enough to make a cape with a hood. I'll cut two slits for the arms, that'll be easy." I held the curtain up to my head.

Mom laughed. "Tomorrow morning, I'll pull out the sewing machine and you can start working on your owl."

Chapter 14

THE NEXT MORNING after breakfast, I cleared off the table. I chose yellow and orange felt for my owl so it would really show up on the green cape. Mom measured me for the arm slits and then cut a piece from the bottom of the curtain for the hood. We worked until noon, and the result was amazing.

"It didn't cost a penny." I gave Mom a big hug. "Thanks for helping me."

At dinnertime, Gram came and brought pizza. I modelled my Owl Power cape and she was impressed. "You two are quite the team."

"Did you talk to people about rentals?" I asked.

Gram's face darkened. "I've talked to people at church, the

choir, at yoga and my book club, but they all give me the same response. There are no rentals in this area."

After Gram left, I took Mom's hand. "We can't give up hope, Mom."

"We won't. We've got Owl Power on our side!" She high-fived me.

That night, I called Frieda and told her about my costume.

"I can't wait to see it. I'm wearing Jacob's green sweater and toque with my shell."

"I wonder what everyone else will be wearing. I'm sure Mr. R. will wear something wacky."

"Did you ask Cedar what he's going to be for Halloween?" my friend asked.

"I never talk to him anymore. He leaves as soon as the last bell rings."

"We'll find out on Friday. I've gotta go, see you tomorrow."

. . .

Bedlam abounded in our classroom on Monday morning. I took my earplugs out of my bag, hoping I wouldn't have an attack.

"Violet! Go sit with Karen!" Brianna yelled. "I know you don't want to sit with me. You want to sit with your real friend." She left her seat and sat at the back of the room. "Don't look at me!" she screamed. "Just so you know, I won't have a costume on Friday because my mother refuses to let me make one from old clothes. The only costume I'm allowed to wear is something new from a store!" Tears streamed down her face.

Mr. R. had watched from the front of the room. We all held our breath when he walked slowly to the back and stopped beside her.

"Brianna, take a deep breath and calm down. Let's all help you before you have a breakdown."

Brianna looked up. "I tried to reduce and recycle but my mom says it's nonsense and it won't help our planet."

I was stunned. How could her mother say that?

"You are very brave, Brianna. You want to help the environment. You're showing responsibility and I'm proud of you. You know, I understand your mom. What we do for the environment as individuals or as a class doesn't seem to make any difference at all. It feels like Mother Earth won't even notice. But if everybody in this class does a little bit and you talk about it at home, then your family will do a little bit, and then you talk to your friends and neighbours. Remember how you make a snowman? You start with a snowball and roll it in the snow. As you roll it, more snow sticks to it and that tiny ball becomes bigger and bigger!" We all nodded. "That's how this works, too. It's called the snowball effect."

I liked that. The snowball effect.

"Remember how climate activist Greta Thunberg sat on the steps of the Swedish Parliament all by herself, with her sign demanding climate action?" Mr. R. continued. "And one year later, she had inspired young people all over the globe to join her in the Fridays for Future climate strike, demanding action from world leaders!"

We spent a week making climate action signs in class this past September, and then parents drove students from our school to Centennial Park on the Friday at lunchtime. From there, we marched over to City Hall. We were not the only school participating. Many parents and grandparents joined the strike. But I also knew that Brianna's mom was not the only adult who didn't believe that we could solve this enormous problem.

"Young people like Greta are the snowball. They inspire us all to demand change," Mr. R. continued. "I'm so proud of all of you because you have proven to me that you're taking these issues seriously." He returned to his desk. "How can we help Brianna?"

"Maybe she should let it go and buy a costume. It's not worth fighting with her mom." Violet surprised us all.

"Thank you, Violet. You make a good point." He sat down.

"I won't get a costume." Brianna stood up. "Can I borrow one? Frieda, can I borrow one of your pink princess costumes?"

"I — Yes, of course." Frieda looked shocked.

"When it comes to problem-solving, you are the best. You all get an A for this challenging test." Mr. R. wrote a giant A on the board.

. . .

On Tuesday, the grade one teacher came into our classroom.

"*What brings you here, Mrs. McTeer?*" our teacher asked.

"Thank you for your kind rhyme. I was wondering whether any of your students have costumes at home that are too small, and whether they would be willing to lend them to some of my students who won't have a costume on Friday. I promise you will get them back after Halloween."

Frieda was the first one to raise her hand. "I have several pink princess gowns I'd like to donate to your students."

After Frieda, almost every student said that they had a costume lying around at home. I would bring my gnome costume tomorrow.

Mrs. McTeer's smile reached all the way to her ears. "Your students are the best, Mr. R."

Our teacher winked at us and pointed at the A on the board.

For the rest of the week, we were busy with research activities related to the origin of Halloween. We brainstormed recipes for homemade treats to bring to the class party on Friday, typed them up and shared them in a booklet. No one in our class had any food allergies, which made it easy.

Before long, Thursday came around.

"Hi Cedar," I said as we got our bikes.

"Hi."

"Do you have a costume for tomorrow?"

"Yup."

"Is tomorrow your last day?"

"Please don't tell the class." He didn't look at me.

"Does Mr. R. know?"

He shook his head and pedalled away. He raced down the street like he was being chased by demons. My eyes teared up as I watched him go. It didn't seem fair that he had to leave.

. . .

Mom and I made no-bake chocolate eyeballs after supper. We used white chocolate and coconut oil for the eyeballs and dark chocolate chips for pupils.

As I lay in bed that night, worries popped in and out of my head. *Please, no panic attacks tomorrow*, I begged myself. *Use your earplugs and visualize the great horned owl, the northern spotted owl and the little one with the glasses, the spectacles.* I was excited about the costumes, the parade through the school and the activities we would do at our class party in the afternoon. But I was sad about Cedar leaving. It took a long time, but eventually, I fell asleep.

Chapter 15

"HERE ARE THE EYEBALLS." Mom placed a cookie tin on the table. I put the container, my lunch and the cape inside my backpack.

Ding-dong. The doorbell, this early? We exchanged a confused glance and went to the window. Joe's station wagon was parked in front of our house.

I ran to open the door. "Morning, Joe."

Joe stared at me, bewildered. His clothes were rumpled and his braid had come undone.

"Come inside," Mom urged. "You look like you could use some coffee."

His eyes filled as he stepped into our kitchen. "It's Cedar."

Suddenly, the wire tightened around my chest. Something bad had happened to Cedar. I knew it.

"What happened?" Mom asked.

"You haven't seen him?" Joe replied.

We both shook our heads.

"He disappeared from his father's place last night around nine."

"But I thought he was going to his dad's after Halloween?" My breath quickened.

"His dad changed plans." Joe wiped his eyes.

"Downtown? He . . . ran away?" I had heard scary stories about downtown at night. People got beat up, or attacked with a knife.

"His father and I have looked all over for him, but no luck." He took a big breath.

"Did you contact the police?" Mom placed a mug of coffee in front of him.

"We called and they're looking for him." He sipped the coffee. "I can't lose him. I'm so proud of that boy."

"You'll find him, Joe. Don't give up hope." Mom patted his hand.

I swallowed the lump in my throat. "I want to help look for Cedar."

"That's a great idea." Mom looked at Joe. "We'll take our bikes and search the neighbourhood. Why don't you call the school, Rebecca."

I punched in the school's phone number.

"This is Rebecca Brooks and I would like to speak to Mr. R., please." I waited.

"Rebecca! Happy Halloween!" He sounded surprised, but as enthusiastic as always.

"Mr. R.," I said, without giving him a chance to ask me why I called. "I'm not coming today. We have an emergency. Cedar is lost and Mom and I are going to help find him."

The line went silent.

"Something has happened to Cedar." I almost choked on my words.

"Please keep me posted." Mr. R.'s voice was soft. "I'll come out as soon as I can find a supply teacher."

"But what about Halloween?" I couldn't believe what he had just said.

"As soon as I can, I'll bike over to Joe's house." Mr. R. hung up. I stared at the receiver.

"He's coming to help look for Cedar." I was shocked.

"How?" Mom asked.

"He's getting a supply teacher," I answered. "I hope Miss Hayes is available. She lives close to the school and she's really nice."

Joe finished his coffee and got up.

"Where should we look?" I asked.

"That's the problem." Joe wiped his mouth on my owl napkin. "We've been everywhere downtown. Cedar's father, Rick, is still searching for him."

"Did he maybe go back to your house?" I asked.

"I haven't been home. I mean, my house is a long way from Rick's place. I came straight here, hoping he would have called you." Joe shook his head. "I don't know why I came here. It's a safe place, I guess."

"I'm glad you came, Joe." Mom patted his shoulder.

"Why would Cedar run away?"

"That's a good question, Rebecca. I thought maybe something had happened, but Rick tells me that nothing happened, that suddenly he was just gone."

I couldn't imagine that Cedar would just leave and not tell his dad. I was sure something had happened.

"Where did you say your son is now?" Mom asked.

"He's my son-in-law," Joe answered. "He told me he would search the trail down by the river."

"We'll help you look for him. Rebecca, go grab our bikes. Joe, you should go home, so there'll be someone there if Cedar returns."

As Joe walked to his car, a cyclist in a bright orange suit raced toward us. He slammed on the brakes and ground to a halt in front of our home. It was such a realistic orangutan costume that I hardly recognized my teacher.

"Sorry," he panted, pointing at his outfit. "I didn't bring any regular clothes." He leaned his bike against the blue gate. "Tell me what happened."

Joe told him what he had told us.

"I went to your house, Joe." He was still catching his breath. "Nobody was home."

"How did you know that Joe was here, Mr. R.?" I asked.

"I didn't, but I knew that Cedar had a special friend in you, and you made the phone call, Rebecca."

My face burned. I didn't think I was that special.

"Let's bike around the neighbourhood," Mom said. "He might have returned to this area, or maybe he got a ride."

"What about the school?" I asked. "If he's hiding, he might have gone to the trails behind the school. There are tons of places to hide there."

"I'll check my house." Joe got into the driver's seat.

"Mom, will you bike the trails with me?"

"Yes, and we'll sweep the neighbourhood on our way to the school." Mom got on her bike.

"I'll check the wooded area beside Joe's property." Mr. R. mounted his bicycle.

"Thanks, Mr. R.," I said, jumping on mine.

"We'll find him, Rebecca. We will."

The streets were empty since school had already started and people had left for work. Jack-o'-lanterns, dangling ghosts and witches on broomsticks all stared at us as we rode by, but I wasn't interested in Halloween anymore. The trails behind our school led into the woods and Cedar often went there. These paths were always busy with dog walkers, cyclists and hikers. There were many places Cedar could hide if he didn't want to be found. We followed the trail that wound behind the school and biked into the woods.

We met a man walking his dog and Mom slowed down.

"Excuse me, have you seen a boy with long hair, about eleven years old?"

"We didn't meet anyone. It's usually quiet this time of the day."

We continued. Several times, I called, "Cedar! Where are you?" But no one answered.

The trail became too muddy to ride our bikes, so we dismounted. At the foot of a small hill, we ditched our bicycles in the shrubs and climbed to the top. From there, we had a full view of the area. Most trees had lost their leaves, so we could see through them. But there was still no sign of my friend.

"Cedar!" Over and over, I called his name. Apart from two crows and a blue jay, there was no response.

"Let's check out the other side of the hill," Mom suggested.

As we made our way down, I noticed a structure at the foot of the hill. Someone had built a shelter out of plywood and other debris. The roof was a slab of sheet metal.

I looked at Mom. "Let's call. If he's inside, we don't want to scare him. Cedar! It's me, Rebecca, and my mom is with me!"

No answer.

We walked around the structure and found the opening. The entrance was covered by a piece of fabric nailed to a two-by-four.

Mom lifted one of the corners. Inside, we saw a dirty sleeping bag, a towel and several cans, but no sign of Cedar.

"It looks like a homeless person's shelter." I shivered and

tried to imagine us living in a place like this.

"You're right," Mom added. "Let's go. I feel like we're trespassing."

Defeated, we walked back, picked up our bikes and pedalled to Finch Street. As Joe's house came into view, a taxi stopped out front. A tall man wearing a baseball cap got out. As he walked up to the house, I noticed him wiping his eyes. Cedar's dad, Rick, I thought.

"Maybe they've found him." I picked up speed and raced to the two bald eagles at the entrance.

Mom followed. We parked our bikes and rang the bell.

Joe opened the door. I could tell by the look in his eyes that Cedar hadn't been found.

"Come in." We followed him to the kitchen. My teacher and the man from the taxi sat at the table.

Mr. R. stood up. "You didn't notice anything behind the school?"

I shook my head.

"This is Cedar's father." Joe pointed to the man with the baseball cap.

"Hi Rebecca. I'm Rick. My son told me about you and the owl project."

I didn't expect that Cedar would tell his father about me. I didn't know what to say. Joe pulled out two chairs and we sat down.

"The police will be here shortly, and then we'll have to decide what needs to happen next." Joe sat down.

"Can they make an announcement on the radio?" I asked.

"We will ask them to send out an alert," Rick answered.

"Did something happen to upset Cedar before he took off?" Mr. R. looked at Rick.

Rick avoided his gaze. One of his eyes twitched and he cracked the knuckles of one hand with the other. He didn't answer my teacher's question. The kitchen fell quiet. My mind raced as I tried frantically to figure out what could have happened between Cedar and his dad and where Cedar might have gone.

Chapter 16

SUDDENLY, I JUMPED UP. "Did anyone check the tree house?" I sprinted out the door without waiting for an answer. I followed the path that Cedar and I had walked just a few weeks ago. At the arbour, the last rose petals had dropped to the ground and blended into the blanket of leaves. I stopped at the foot of the large maple tree. The canopy of leaves that had hidden the structure from sight had all been blown down by the wind.

I hesitated. Should I call? Step by step, I climbed the rungs until I stood in front of the door. I knocked. No answer. I knocked louder. "Cedar!" I tried the door, but it was locked. "Cedar! Are you in there? Please open the door?"

"Go away, Rebecca!"

The knot in my stomach evaporated. He was safe. "Everybody is looking for you! We're worried. Your grandfather is very upset!"

Cedar didn't respond. I waited. After a while, I heard a noise. The lock turned and the door opened a crack.

"Come in." He closed the door behind me and we stood facing each other. I could tell that he'd been crying.

"How did you get here?"

"I walked all night."

"All the way from downtown?"

Cedar nodded.

"What happened?"

"Did they call the police?" He looked terrified.

"Yes, but they're not here. Do you know who else helped look for you? Mr. R."

Fresh tears rolled down his cheeks. When he wiped them on his sleeve, I didn't know where to look. He slumped onto the bench, grabbed the blanket that was on the floor, wrapped it around his shoulders and buried his head in his hands. "They'll arrest me," he sobbed. "I'll go to jail."

"But you didn't do anything! You're not going to jail!" What was he talking about? "Just because your dad was in jail doesn't mean that you're going, too." Confused, frustrated and a little angry, I sat down on the bench across from him.

Cedar looked up. "Remember, I told you my father did drugs?"

"Yes."

"He promised me that he would quit if I came to live with him. Last night, he was sleeping on the couch in front of the TV, and someone knocked on the door."

My heartbeat was in my throat. I knew this was not going to be good.

"I opened the door and there stood this giant of a man. He had a bald head, pierced ears and tattoos all over his arms. I got really scared and freaked out." Cedar swallowed. "He asked if I was Rick's son. Well, he kind of growled it. I nodded, and he handed me a package and said, 'I need the money right now.'"

"What did you do? Didn't your dad wake up?"

"I couldn't think straight, but as soon as he stepped inside, I dove under his arm and ran out the door. I kept running until my feet wouldn't go anymore. I had no idea where I was, but I still had the package. All I could think of was getting away. If that guy got a hold of me, he'd have killed me. He probably killed my dad when I left because I knew he didn't have enough money to pay for the drugs. I was just scared and didn't know what to do. I even got lost in the dark. I took a long way to get back here."

I didn't know what to say. The whole situation was too big for me to grasp.

"Rebecca! Cedar!" I heard Mom and Mr. R. calling.

"Where is the package now?" I asked.

"I still have it," he whispered.

"I'll tell them that you're safe." I stood up and opened the door. "We'll be right there," I called down. "Cedar is safe. He needs a few more minutes. Did the police come?"

"Oh, thank goodness. They're not here yet, but we'll let them know that Cedar has been found." Mom smiled at me. "Are you alright, Rebecca?"

"Yes, and Cedar is, too." I closed the door. "Come." I reached for his arm.

Cedar let the blanket slide off his shoulders as he stood.

"Your grandfather will be so relieved."

I opened the door and climbed down the ladder. Cedar followed.

Just before we reached the house, he asked, "Is my dad in there?"

"Yes. Your father didn't die, he's been searching for you all night."

I opened the door and Cedar walked into the kitchen with his head down. Everybody still sat around the table. Joe immediately got up and threw his arms around his grandson as tears streamed down his face.

Rick was next. He stood up and looked at his son, but Cedar didn't run into his arms.

"You promised," Cedar said. "You promised, but you lied. You were never planning on quitting!" His voice was raw, his fists clenched. His father looked down and came no closer. Tears ran down Cedar's face.

"This is for the family to deal with, Rebecca. Come, we need to go." Mom stood up and took my hand.

Mr. R. rose from his chair, too. He placed his hand on Cedar's shoulder. "Glad you're safe."

Without a word, we left the house and grabbed our bikes. At our street, my teacher turned right, waved and pedalled back to school. Mom and I went home.

I felt relieved but sad for Cedar. His dad had broken his promise and betrayed his trust.

"People who are addicted can't just quit," Mom said when we sat at the kitchen table. I wondered what would happen to Cedar now.

Chapter 17

I TOLD MOM WHAT Cedar had told me and about the package that he still had. "Could the police arrest him for having drugs?"

"If he tells them the truth and hands them the package, I'm sure he won't get arrested."

I rested my chin in my hands, reflecting on the events of this very different Halloween.

"You can still go to school for a few hours, if you want to."

I shook my head. "I don't feel like partying."

"I get that. Come, let's eat lunch." Mom took some eggs out of the fridge and cracked them into the frying pan.

"We should look for rentals after. Or . . . you could tell me about my father."

Mom froze. She turned away from the stove and faced me.

"I know you have a right to know." She looked away. "It won't be easy to understand. You're still so young."

"But I could try, if you give me a chance."

Mom turned off the burner. "What do you want to know?"

"I want you to tell me why my dad is in Australia. Why do you never want to talk about him? Why doesn't he know about me? And why can I not see him?"

Mom spun her ring around and around. She took a deep breath. "I don't know where to begin."

"At the beginning."

She pulled out a chair and sat down beside me.

"When I was nineteen, I made a huge mistake." Mom paused.

I knew my mother was nineteen when I was born. "Was I the huge mistake?"

"No, no! Never think that. You're the best thing that has ever happened to me. I don't know what I'd do without you." Her face was wet, her nose runny.

"It doesn't matter. Don't we all do things that we regret later? Just like when I called Cedar weird and didn't want to work with him?"

Mom folded her hands and took a deep breath. "I'll tell you a story about a girl who had big dreams and loved life, and thought nothing bad could happen to her."

"Keep going," I urged. The sooner she told me the truth, the better.

"The summer of my nineteenth birthday, I published my first magazine article and fell hopelessly in love with a young man from Australia. He was staying with our neighbours for the months of July and August." She stared at her hands. I waited.

"The neighbours' daughter was my best friend. She, her older brother, the Australian man and I did everything together that summer." Mom rubbed her arms. "The four of us hiked, went swimming, went to the movies and, on some weekends, went camping. I knew he liked me because he always walked beside me, rode his bike beside mine and sat next to me in the movie theatre." Mom got up and put the kettle on. "He went home the last weekend of August. It was the end of an unforgettable summer. The night before he left, we said goodbye. I promised I would write to him and maybe, one day, visit him in Australia. I was so naïve."

"What was so naïve about wanting to write to him?"

"Well, he told me that he didn't want me to write to him. He was planning to marry his high school sweetheart that fall."

"Oh, Mom. That was mean."

"Maybe if he had told me that at the beginning of the summer, we would have just been friends instead." She sighed. "A few weeks after he left, I discovered I was pregnant."

I felt my chest tighten. This story was so different from what I had imagined.

"I thought maybe my father had died and you didn't want

to tell me, so you made up the story about him living in Australia."

Mom placed her hand over mine. "I didn't make it up, Rebecca. I couldn't tell you because I didn't think you would understand. I was afraid you would judge me. I didn't want to tell him because he was getting married and that would make things complicated for him."

"But what about you? Didn't your life become complicated?"

"That was my choice, Rebecca. What if I had told him and he wanted you to come to Australia?"

"Could he have asked that from you?"

"Probably not, but I didn't want to take the chance. I wanted to keep you all to myself."

"What if I want to contact him? Will you stop me?"

"I will for now. But I guess when you're eighteen, you won't need my permission."

"Will you at least tell me his name?"

"No, because I don't want you to search for him on the internet."

"Did you look him up on the internet?"

"No."

"Why not?"

"I don't want to know." Mom stared out the window.

"Did you ever regret your decision?"

"No." Mom smiled a thin smile.

"What happened to your best friend? Do you still see her?"

Mom shook her head. "She moved to New Zealand and we lost touch. At the time, I was too embarrassed to tell her."

I didn't know how to respond.

"The day you were born, Gram gave me this." Mom took off her ring and gave it to me. "This ring belonged to my grandmother."

I turned the stone toward the light and a thousand colours sparkled in the white opal. Mom always wore it, but I'd never heard its history.

I stared at the ring. My head was heavy with all the questions I was afraid to ask. This was all so new, so strange, and not at all what I had expected. I needed to sort through everything she'd told me.

Mom wiped her eyes. "I wasn't going to tell you until you were older, but after everything you've experienced today, I couldn't turn you away again. You're more grown up than any other eleven-year-old and I know you will always support me."

I gave Mom a big hug and told her I wanted to be alone for a while. I went to my room and lay down on my bed. Having a father was no longer some vague notion. My dad was *real*, and I needed to get used to him, even though I wasn't going to meet him any time soon.

· · ·

Later, Mom and I checked for rentals. There were none except for a big old house that Mom couldn't afford.

Mom hugged me tight. "Are you alright, now that you know about your father?"

I hugged her back. "I have a lot to think about."

"I know." Mom kissed my hair.

Frieda called just before supper. She asked why I wasn't in class and mentioned that Mr. R. had come in late, which was odd because he was so excited for Halloween. I told her about our morning adventure.

"Wow. That's really intense. Thank goodness you found him." There was a long pause. "I missed you at the party, but will you at least come trick-or-treating with me tonight?"

"Frieda's asking if I can go trick-or-treating with her."

"Sure," Mom answered.

"We still have the eyeballs we made for class, can we give them to trick-or-treaters?"

"No, we'll have to eat them because they're homemade. So many kids have allergies. We have those store-bought mini bars, they have the ingredients listed on the wrapper."

I found the box and put the treats in a basket by the door. We made soup for dinner, but the doorbell rang as soon as we sat down. Two bunnies and a big black cat sang, "Trick or treat, trick or treat, will you give us something sweet?"

I quickly slipped into my Owl Power cape. The trio started giggling and accepted the sweets.

My BFF picked me up at 6:30. Her turtle costume looked amazing. She told me about the party and asked how Cedar was.

"He was upset and scared. I don't know what will happen next."

"It's very sad for him. I hope he stays with his grandfather."

I agreed.

"You won't believe what Brianna did! She thanked me for the costume and gave me a present."

"What?" My jaw dropped.

"She made me a stuffed seal out of old jeans for my seal collection. It's decorated with beads and she embroidered the seal with seaweed, tiny fish and shells. It's gorgeous. She's so talented. I didn't know what to say. It's the most special gift I've ever received." I raised my eyebrows, and she blushed. "Oh . . . I'm sorry. The seals you gave me are very special, too."

"Just remember that I'm your BFF and she's your former enemy." I winked and gave her a hug.

Frieda smiled back. "That's what makes this gift so amazing."

Without realizing it, we had walked all the way down our street without stopping to ring a single doorbell.

"Hey, we need to get serious about trick-or-treating!" She stopped in her tracks. "This could be our last time. Next year, when we're twelve, we'll be too old." She grabbed my arms and shook them until we both burst out laughing. The tension and frustration I'd felt about Cedar and my dad dissipated. After a while, we caught our breath and started trick-or-treating like it was our last time.

Chapter 18

CEDAR WASN'T AT school on the Monday after Halloween. I had wanted to call him over the weekend, but Mom told me to wait and give him time.

The classroom buzzed with excitement. Mr. R. was about to announce our new assignment for environmental studies. As always, his T-shirt gave away the topic.

"Trees! The most important living things for Mother Earth." He pointed at his shirt. "*You may work in groups of two or more, but the maximum number of students is four.*"

I caught Frieda's eye. She was already inching her chair closer to me.

"Cedar would have liked this topic, don't you think? His house is surrounded by trees."

"We could ask one more person and if Cedar shows up in the next few days, he can join our group," Frieda suggested.

"If he wants to work with us. Who else should we ask?" I looked around the room. Brianna was the only one who wasn't part of a group. I didn't really want to work with her and I was sure Frieda felt the same. Still, she looked very lonely.

When Mr. R. came around to check on the groups, I asked, "What will we do about the waiting list for baby owls?"

"Good question," he answered. "I'll write it on the board so we won't forget to discuss it before you go home today."

I waved at Brianna and motioned for her to come over. She looked at our teacher, who nodded his approval and winked at us. She picked up her chair, walked over to our table and sat down.

"Frieda told me about the beautiful seal you made," I said to break the ice. Brianna smiled.

"If or when Cedar comes back to school, he can work with us, too." Frieda looked at Brianna, who stayed silent. "You can talk. Just don't get too bossy."

"And you can't be mean," I added.

"Okay. I won't. I promise." Brianna smiled at both of us.

We made a list of all the benefits of trees. It was actually fun, and the day flew by. Just before the bell, Mr. R. organized a brainstorm session about our next owl sale. Everyone stocked up on materials so we could sew more owlets at home. We would also have time in class to work on them. Our sale was planned for the last Friday in November.

On the way home, I stopped by Frieda's for a few minutes to admire the seal Brianna gave her.

"It's definitely a piece of art." I traced the beads with my finger.

"I feel bad for her." Frieda took the seal from me and placed it on her bookshelf beside the other two stuffies. "We should invite her to hang out once in a while."

"Not too often." I admired a conch shell she used as a bookend.

Frieda chuckled. "We'll start slowly and see how it goes."

As soon as I got home, I told Mom about our plans for the next sale. "I hope we can make another hundred baby owls."

She put a glass of milk and a plate of cookies on the table. "I'll help. And once Gram's settled into her new place, I'm sure she'll pitch in, too."

"I'd love it if we could adopt all twelve endangered species. Then every team in my class would get a certificate and a stuffy."

"That's a lot of money."

"I know it's not going to happen. We could never sew that many owls. But it would be amazing."

Our conversation continued while Mom cooked pasta and I sliced tomatoes and peppers. When everything was on the stove, I took out my homework. Mom brought her laptop to the table and we worked side by side until dinner was ready.

. . .

After we finished eating, Joe called and invited us to come over. Mom finished typing one more paragraph and then we grabbed our jackets and fetched our bikes from the shed. The streets were quiet. Remnants of Halloween decor swayed from porches.

A knot formed in my stomach as we rode down the street. I knew Cedar and Joe had important news, or they wouldn't have invited us. We parked our bikes in their yard and the front door opened before we had a chance to ring the bell.

"Glad you could come." Joe ushered us into the hallway and took our jackets. "Cedar is in the kitchen, making tea."

The bright, open rooms and the smell of wood calmed my nerves. I entered the kitchen, where Cedar stood hunched by the table.

"Hi." I smiled slightly.

He kept his head down and placed four mugs on the table.

"I've asked you to come because I don't know what to do with Cedar." Joe pulled out some chairs for us. "He doesn't want to go back to school."

"I do want to go back," Cedar said softly. "I just can't face the students, or Mr. R. I'm so embarrassed."

"You don't need to be embarrassed." I sat down. "What you went through was terrible."

"But I messed up. I made the wrong choices. You all had to look for me. I was so scared I couldn't think straight."

I didn't know what to say, but Mom jumped in. "Nobody could have prepared you for what happened, Cedar. That was not a normal situation for someone your age to be in, or for anybody. It's understandable that you didn't know what to do."

"I've told him that, too, but I can't convince him." Joe wiped his eyes.

"We're studying trees for our next project." I hoped that would get his attention. "Frieda, Brianna and I saved a spot for you in our group, if you'd like to work with us."

He stared wordlessly at his hands.

"Are you staying here?" I asked.

Cedar nodded. "My dad is going into rehab. It's a place on the mainland where they'll help him get off the drugs."

"Being a drug addict is like having a disease," Joe explained.

"Oh." I knew being addicted was difficult, but I didn't know it was a disease. "I hope he gets better."

"We all do." Joe took the teapot from the counter and poured tea into the mugs. "Elderberry!"

The sweetness of the berry tea filled the kitchen. It reminded me of summer.

"What happened to the package that man gave you?" I finally asked. The question had been on my mind since Cedar told me the story.

"The police took it. They were glad Cedar saved it for them, even though running away with the drugs put his life in danger." Joe blew his nose. "The police knew who the dealer was based on Cedar's description of him."

"Will you come to school tomorrow?" I asked as we sipped our tea.

"Yes, I'll come. Thank you both for looking for me. You missed the Halloween party because of me."

"I didn't feel like partying when I heard you were lost."

"I'm carving an eagle for Mr. R."

"He'll like that."

We finished our tea, and Mom and I said goodbye. The sky was dark, but the streetlights showed the way home.

I opened the blue gate. "I'm glad we went to see him." We stored our bicycles in the shed.

"It will be hard for Cedar to face Mr. R. at school tomorrow, and to deal with everyone wondering where he's been." Mom turned the key and opened the front door.

"He's embarrassed that he drew so much attention," I added. "But he shouldn't be, because now he has a ton of friends."

Chapter 19

IN THE WEEK leading up to our sale, our classroom became an owl-making factory. Donations flooded in, even from other teachers and students from other grades. Pieces of felt and containers of buttons and beads covered one of the tables. Embroidery floss, lace and ribbon covered another. Bags of stuffing littered the floor.

Whenever we had free time or finished our assignments early, we worked on the owls. Some students even worked during recess and after lunch. By Friday morning, we counted 150 felt owls for our big lunchtime sale.

"I can't believe we've made so many!" My heart fluttered.

"With the money from the last sale, we'll make $810 if we sell them all."

"If we raise that much, maybe we can sponsor more than our twelve endangered species," Brianna suggested.

I was sure Brianna had made more owls than any of us. Every little owl she made was amazing, and every face had a distinct personality.

"Let's hope so, Brianna!" Mr. R. cleared off his desk. "Okay, let's eat lunch in the classroom before the crowds arrive."

Even before the sale started, students were lined up outside our door. Just like the first time, we displayed our owls in a long line so customers could easily choose their owlet. Half an hour later, we were once again completely sold out.

Our teacher beamed. He wiped his eyes. "This calls for a celebration!" He danced over to the music centre and played his favourite reggae music. We all knew the music, and we all knew the musician, Bob Marley, who was from Mr. R.'s home country, Jamaica. I pulled out my earplugs, but my teacher stopped me. "I promise I won't blast it too loud. If you help me move the tables and chairs, we can all dance!"

"He's so crazy. Look at him dance." Frieda pointed and copied his moves. Soon, we all copied Mr. R.'s dance moves. Even Cedar had a smile on his face as he grooved to the beat.

When the music stopped, it was time to talk business.

"Should we divide the money between the groups or decide together which species we should adopt?" asked Frieda.

"Do we have enough to adopt all twelve?" I asked.

"And if not, how should we decide?" asked Brianna.

"We could put all the animals' names in the hat and Mrs. Kahn could do a draw," Violet suggested. "Karen and I would really like to donate some money to Hannah Bywater's foundation. You can buy a wooden turtle to support sea turtle conservation."

"You are the most amazing and inventive problem solvers," Mr. R. sang. "But this time, I might have the solution. We had twelve presentations, so for each team to have $100, we would need $1200 total." He opened his backpack and pulled out a cheque book. "I'm so proud of you all, and I would love to donate some of my own money to help you save these species. You can spend the money to support one or several endangered species."

Spontaneous applause erupted. The students went wild. The stomping, table banging and screeching hit my brain. Oh, no. A *thunderbolt* was about to hit me. This time, though, I was ready to fight back. I put in the earplugs, covered my ears, closed my eyes and went to my magical place where the great horned owl swooped down on silent wings to land on my arm. When I could feel its soft feathers and see its long talons, its sharp beak and beady eyes, I heard it screech, "You're fine, you're fine, you're fine." My breathing stabilized.

"Rebecca! Rebecca!" Frieda shook my arm. "It's quiet. Open your eyes. Take out your earplugs. Everyone is quiet."

I opened my eyes and removed the plugs. Everyone was staring at me. A grin took over my face.

"It worked." I could hardly believe it. This was the first time.

"What worked?" Frieda asked.

"The earplugs helped a little bit, but when I visualized the great horned owl landing on my arm, I could breathe."

"Great work, Rebecca." Mr. R.'s eyes shone. "You are amazing!"

I felt so good. For the first time in my life, I had prevented a panic attack. It felt like I'd defeated a monster before it could destroy me. I relaxed in my seat, totally calm and happy.

"Before I give you time to discuss the adoption kit for your endangered species, I want to say something." Mr. R. looked at all of us. *"Young people all around the world are getting smart. They won't wait for politicians or governments to do their part."* He opened his laptop. "I'll show you a few short videos of youth who are already making a huge difference in protecting the environment. These kids are an inspiration to us all."

First, he showed us a video of Hannah Bywater, who was trying to save sea turtles and orangutans. Next, we listened to Greta Thunberg, the Swedish climate activist who addressed the United Nations and was nominated for the Nobel Peace Prize. We also watched a clip of the video in which she crossed the Atlantic Ocean in a zero-emissions yacht.

"I admire all the young activists." I nudged my BFF. "But Greta is one of my all-time heroes."

"*Young people will lead the way to a future where all species have a chance to stay,*" our teacher rhymed after we'd watched all of the videos.

For the last part of the afternoon, we printed and filled out application forms for our endangered species. Cedar and I decided to adopt five northern spotted owl eggs, even though we would need to wait until spring.

"We'll make a list of all the organizations for the species you want to sponsor or adopt. I will write a cheque for each team," Mr. R. announced when it was time to go home.

One by one, we thanked our teacher and filed out into the hallway. I noticed that Cedar stayed behind. He took something from his backpack. I wanted to watch, but I didn't. This was Cedar's moment to thank Mr. R. I knew he had finished the eagle he told me about last week, but I hadn't seen it.

I waited for him by the school gate. When he finally left the building and walked down to his bicycle, he hopped on and screeched to a halt right beside me.

"Did he like the eagle?" I asked.

A smile lit up his face. "He said it was the most treasured piece of art that he would ever own. And that even when I become a successful artist, he will always remember me as the boy who ran away and made him ride his bike all over town in his orangutan costume."

"Oh, Cedar. That is so like Mr. R." I laughed. "I'm surprised he didn't speak in rhyme."

Cedar laughed. We mounted our bikes and rode side by

side. Before he turned onto his street, he paused. "Thanks for being my friend, Rebecca."

I didn't know what to say. All I could do was smile at him and bike home.

. . .

"Everything is almost perfect, Mom." I put on the kettle. I told her about the successful owl sale, the cheques and Cedar's eagle. Then I told her how I had prevented my latest panic attack.

"I put my earplugs in and closed my eyes. I imagined I was back at The Raptors with you, Joe and Cedar. I watched Jim the falconer disappear behind the trees with the owl perched on his arm. I waited for Talia to give the signal. I held my breath and stared as that wondrous creature soared toward me without a sound. I remembered the jolt on my arm as it landed, its soft feathers against my face, and its orange eyes looking at me. I heard it screech, 'You're fine, you're fine,' and my breathing slowed down. I felt the magic, just like that afternoon. My heart stopped pounding, my breathing found its rhythm and the tightness in my chest eased. The great horned owl saved me."

Mom jumped up and hugged me. "I'm so proud of you, Rebecca. Now that you've succeeded once, it can happen again. It might not work every time, but at least you know you can do it."

Mom sat down and I sliced some apples. "Only one more thing could make this day, and our lives, perfect."

"If we found a place to live." She patted my shoulder. "Remember, life is never perfect, but you came close today."

"Right."

"You know, you're not the only one who had a good day." Mom poured tea into two owl mugs.

"Really? Don't leave me hanging!"

"My publisher phoned. They'll take my vampire story, on one condition."

"What's the condition?"

"They want a series of three books."

"Is that good? Will you do it? I mean, can you write two more books about vampires?"

"Yes, yes! Of course, I said yes!" Mom pulled me off the chair, threw her arms around me and lifted me off the ground. "I don't know for sure if I can do it, but I'll try very hard, and I'll make the stories about the environment." She put me down. "You have inspired me to write about endangered species . . . and endangered vampires."

"You can do it, Mom. I know you can! What a brilliant, nearly perfect day."

She hugged me tight. "As my dad would say, for every problem . . ."

"There is a solution."

Chapter 20

DING-DONG. We both jumped, and I ran to the window. A black car was parked in front of our house. Mom ran into the hallway and I followed closely. She opened the door.

"Mr. Wong."

I had only met Mr. Wong once before. He wore a long black coat and a black-and-grey striped toque.

"Come in." Mom stepped back. "We've just made tea. Do you remember Rebecca?"

"Hello, Rebecca," he said with a heavy accent.

"I hope you aren't bringing us bad news." Mom offered him a chair.

"Yes and no." Mr. Wong removed his toque. He took several deep breaths, as though he had run all the way instead of driving his car.

"What's the bad news?" Mom wrung her hands. I grabbed the back of a chair and waited.

"You don't have to move out on December 31st," he answered.

"Has the sale been postponed?" Mom asked.

"The deal fell through. It was a bad deal. There is no sale." Mr. Wong twisted his toque around in his hands.

My thoughts raced. What did this mean?

"We can stay?" I asked.

"I wish for you to stay." Mr. Wong looked at me. "But have no choice. I need money. Have to sell the house."

"What if nobody will buy it?" Mom asked.

I grabbed her hands. "Mom! Mom! We can buy it! The book deal, Mom! You said you'd write the vampire trilogy! You'll have money!" I shook her hands up and down. "Will the money be enough?"

"Yes, I think it would be enough for a down payment. But Rebecca, I haven't signed a contract yet."

"But you will, right? And you'll get money when you sign?" My breathing accelerated, but I stayed focused. For a moment, I forgot about Mr. Wong, who was staring at us. I released Mom's hands and faced him, standing up a little straighter. "Mr. Wong, we would like to buy the house."

"Rebecca!" Mom clasped her hands. Tears filled her eyes.

"Mr. Wong, Rebecca is right. We would like to buy this house." She wiped her face on her sleeve and wrapped her arms around me.

"Wow!" Mr. Wong said. "So happy for you. Yes, I like selling the house to you and Rebecca." He stood up.

"I don't know how much money I'll have, and we'll have to get a mortgage. It's all so sudden. I just talked to my publisher today." Mom stood behind me and rubbed my shoulders. Excitement and happiness bubbled inside me. I barely managed to hold in a squeal.

"I'll make an appointment with my lawyer. It will all work out for you, and for me." Mr. Wong shook Mom's hand. "And also for you," he said, shaking mine. We all laughed with relief.

As soon as Mr. Wong left, I leapt into Mom's arms. We both cried and laughed as she twirled me around the table.

"This is a perfect day! We have a place to live forever! I'll call Gram, and Frieda and Cedar!" I ran to the phone, dialled Gram's number and told her everything in one breath. She was beyond excited.

"Gram says she'll come over as soon as possible." I hung up and danced around the kitchen table.

"I hope she brings ice cream to celebrate." Mom couldn't stop smiling.

"Your favourite this time," I added.

After I told everybody the amazing news, I wanted to run into our street and yell that we were *not* moving at the end of

December. Mom laughed and suggested that we tell the neighbours directly instead of screaming it into the night.

Moments later, Frieda arrived. "I'm sooooo happy you're not moving." She gave me one of her great big bear hugs, then she hugged my mom. "I brought sweet potato chips and salsa." She opened her backpack and took out the treats. I grabbed a bowl for the chips.

"I'll cut some carrots and cucumber." Mom opened the fridge. "And we have freshly made hummus, too."

Frieda placed the chips and salsa on the table. "I'm glad your gram is coming to the party. She's so cool."

"I guess we *are* having a party." I laughed and added glasses for drinks and bowls for ice cream.

Gram arrived just as Cedar and Joe pulled up.

"Wow, I didn't realize you were coming, too." I waved them into the house.

Gram hugged us and I introduced her to Cedar and his grandfather. As I hoped, she handed Mom her favourite ice cream, pralines and cream. Cedar and Joe brought an apple cinnamon cake.

"Did you bake it?" I asked.

"Gramma's recipe. We make one every Friday, just like she used to do."

"I invited someone else," Frieda confessed when we were finally sitting around the table.

"The more the merrier." Mom's eyes sparkled.

"Who is it?" I asked.

"You'll see," Frieda answered. She looked out the window.

"Oh, he's here!" She ran to the door to welcome the guest. It was Mr. R!

As he took off his jacket, he rhymed, *"I felt it would be a terrible disgrace, if I missed the party at Rebecca's place."*

We all applauded.

"Thank you for coming." I couldn't believe everyone was here to celebrate with us.

"I'm thrilled to be invited! Where can I play my music?" He took a CD from his backpack. "We can't party without music."

I squeezed Mom's arm. "This is so amazing. I can hardly believe this is happening."

Mom teared up as she turned to our guests. "I'm so happy you all came to help Rebecca and me celebrate our good news."

Soon, reggae music filled our little house. Conversations about vampires, the successful felt owl sales, the adoption of endangered species and the house abounded. Suddenly, my chest tightened. The laughter, the talking and the music made the room grow smaller and smaller until I had no space left to breathe. I pressed my hand against my chest to stop the pain. *No! No! Not now!*

Suddenly, Frieda grabbed my arm. "Stop the music! Stop talking!" she yelled over the noise.

The music stopped and the voices silenced.

I looked around the room at my mom, Gram, my BFF, Cedar, Joe and Mr. R. I was surrounded by family, friends and my favourite teacher. In the silence, I found focus. I listened hard for my screeching mantra. *You're fine, you're fine, you're fine.* Then, as though the great horned owl took off from within my mind, I heard the flutter of wings. My breath found its rhythm and I felt strong. I stood up straight.

"Hey *thunderbolt!*" I declared. "You were NOT invited to this party!"

Mom threw her arms around me and squeezed me tight.

"I'm fine. Let's party, but Mr. R., could you please turn the music down?"

"Sorry Rebecca, I got carried away by the excitement of this incredible day." He crossed his arms and bowed his head.

"No, it wasn't your fault. I was just overwhelmed by everything happening so fast. We had the perfect day at school, Mom got her three-book deal, we're buying the house and everyone came over to party."

The room was quiet for a few seconds, then Joe got up. "We are so glad you're not moving. Remember, if you ever need help, Cedar and I are here for you."

"Thank you for your kindness and friendship Joe, Cedar." Mom smiled.

"You can count on me, too, for whatever you need," my teacher added. *"I'll bike over and help you, guaranteed!"*

Frieda squeezed my hand and I squeezed back.

Gram blew her nose. Mom wiped her eyes. And I felt warm inside.

When all the food was eaten and everyone left, I went over to Mom and hugged her tightly. "This was a totally awesome, PERFECT day!"

AUTHOR'S NOTE

This book is a work of fiction. The characters and places were all made up by the author, except for The Raptors in Duncan, B.C. All of the events happening in this novel were modified to suit the story.

I followed the incredible journey of Greta Thunberg, the Swedish climate activist. When you type Greta's name into your search engine, you will find videos about her actions and her speeches.

You can find information on endangered species and on Hannah Bywater, the young activist, on the internet.

To help you with your research, I have included the following websites:

- pnwraptors.com
  This is the site for the birds of prey education centre in Duncan, B.C.

- nsobreedingprogram.com
  This is the northern spotted owl breeding facility in Langley, B.C., where you can sponsor a spotted owl and adopt an egg.

- defenders.org
  At this site, you can adopt an animal to support protection, research, education and conservation.

- 4ocean.com
  At this site, you'll learn about the Hawaiian monk seal and how you can help by buying a bracelet made from one pound of ocean trash.

- hannahsplanet.ca
  Through this website, you can support sea turtles and
  orangutans.

- worldwildlife.org
  This organization fights for wilderness preservation and the
  reduction of human impact on the environment. They offer
  several adoption programs.

- janegoodall.org
  This takes you to the Jane Goodall Institute, an organization
  that protects wildlife and empowers people.

ABOUT THE AUTHOR

Teaching her grade one students about endangered species inspired Martha to write *Awesome Wildlife Defenders*, a story about young activists, friendships, family and mental health.

Her concern for the environment is reflected in her lifestyle and her writing. She strives to minimize her carbon footprint and lives in an off-grid straw bale home in Powassan, Ontario.

She was born in the Netherlands after the Second World War and her war novels for children and young adults are based on family experiences and historical facts.

Martha's YA novel, *A Time to Choose*, won the Blue Heron Book Award and was shortlisted for the Geoffrey Bilson Award for Historical Fiction. *Hero*, a middle-grade reader, won the Elementary Teachers' Federation of Ontario Writer's Award and was nominated for the Silver Birch Award. *Hero* has been translated into the Frisian language by the Dutch publisher, De Afûk.

As a retired teacher, Martha enjoys working with students, giving school and library presentations and writing stories about the environment and WWII.

You can find more information at her website: www.marthaattema.com